Kinsman of the Gun

Cheyenne, 1888. Ezra McPherson is a gunfighter who cannot escape the past, and Luke Tisdale is a young doctor whose brother has been murdered. Marcus Stokesbury and Eloise Endicott are journalists who are intrigued by the mystery surrounding Ezra. Together with Richard Swearingen, a cattle baron who seeks to establish a kingdom in Wyoming, and Andrew Swearingen, a man who has killed but who is now willing to take an extraordinary step to prevent bloodshed, they all become embroiled in a story of love, greed, betrayal and sacrifice.

Kinsman of the Gun

Walton Young

A Black Horse Western

ROBERT HALE

© Walton Young 2019
First published in Great Britain 2019

ISBN 978-0-7198-2933-8

The Crowood Press
The Stable Block
Crowood Lane
Ramsbury
Marlborough
Wiltshire SN8 2HR

www.bhwesterns.com

Robert Hale is an imprint
of The Crowood Press

The right of Walton Young to be identified as
author of this work has been asserted by him
in accordance with the Copyright, Designs and
Patents Act 1988

This novel is dedicated to my wife, Suzanne

Typeset by
Derek Doyle & Associates, Shaw Heath
Printed and bound in Great Britain by
4Bind Ltd, Stevenage, SG1 2XT

CHAPTER 1

Ginevra Swearingen stood on the parched grassy hilltop overlooking the Medicine Bow River. Lightning streaked across the black Wyoming sky, yet there was no thunder. There was no rain. Only moments ago Ezra McPherson had stood beside her and held her and told her not to be afraid. The dry-weather lightning would not reach them.

Now he was gone. He had returned to Cheyenne. She longed for his touch. She wanted to be held again by the man she had believed was dead. He looked so much older. He probably thought the same thing about her. The lines in his face were deeper. The hair and mustache were gray. Strength clung to him, as it always had, and from the strength he exuded comfort. His hands were hard, but they held hers with a gentleness she had felt from no one else. Somehow, when he was with her, she did not worry about how things would turn out. He would make things right. She believed him – the lightning would not touch her.

'Lightning, come again! I'm not afraid of you! Can you turn back time?'

She stood, alone, and waited for the lightning to answer, but no answer came. In the darkness above the distant mountains, the lightning curled up and refused to appear.

'Can you turn back time? What's the matter? I'm not

5

afraid of you. Are you afraid of me?'

She called louder. Still, no reply came. And she dropped to the hilltop and stared at the mountains. No, not even Ezra could make things right, not this time.

'My son. A killer.'

If the lightning could burn away the present, she could keep her younger son, Andrew, from living a life defined by the Colt on his hip. She could prevent him from going to the Two Rivers Saloon and shooting and killing a man. And she could do more. She could prevent him from lynching a man. Ezra told her about the lynching. She knew he did not want to tell her, but he had to. He wanted to help, and this was all the help he could give. The sheriff would come for her son. Andrew had to leave Wyoming and never return. The shooting in the Two Rivers was called self-defense. Lynching was something else.

'I will make Andrew go to California. He may not want to listen, but he'll have to. I have money. I'll give it to him. He can start a new life. The law won't look for him there.'

She thought about the mother who tonight mourned a son who had died at the end of a rope. She wondered who she was, who the boy was. She wondered what he could have done to deserve such a fate. Probably nothing. Why would Andrew have done such a thing?

'His father, Richard. He is responsible. I blame him. No, I blame me. I was too weak to stand up against Richard. I let him destroy our son. But Ezra has told me what I must do, and I will do it. There is still time to save him.'

She stood and looked at the faraway mountains one last time. She went to her mare and rode down the hill and left the Medicine Bow behind her.

At the edge of Cheyenne, Ezra reined in the stallion beside the city cemetery. He stared at the dark monuments and thought how things don't work out the way you planned. John Tisdale, Luke's brother, would not be returning to the East for burial. He would be buried here in the cemetery at two o'clock in the afternoon. The young woman who was John's friend, and perhaps much more, had convinced Luke that burial here in Cheyenne was the right thing to do. It was what John would have wanted. She seemed to know what she was talking about, and Luke believed her. For that matter, so did Ezra.

Her name was Meta Anderson, and she reminded Ezra so much of Ginevra many years ago. It wasn't just the brown eyes. It was the desire they had to escape the West. Ginevra did not want to live her life on a farm. The city called, and she heard.

Perhaps I should have gone with her, he said to himself. But what could I do in a city?

And then there was the small matter of the war. It was over, at least for many folks, but not for him, not for Jesse, not for Frank. There was a time when Ezra thought it would never be over, but one day he realized it was. The killing had to stop. By then Ginevra was gone, and he figured he would never see her again.

Ezra left the cemetery and rode to the livery. Old Smitty limped out of the darkness of one of the stalls.

'I figured you'd be in bed,' Ezra said.

'I like to check on the gents and ladies that call this livery home. I'll brush this fellow down. Isn't he something special?'

'That he is. I might decide to buy him if you'll sell him.'

'I wouldn't sell him to just anybody. It's got to be someone who knows horses, and I can tell you know them. If you want him, let me know. I'll make a fair deal.'

'I trust you. I'll let you know.'

'By the way, one of your friends has been looking for

7

you. It ain't none of my business, but he seemed awfully concerned.'

'Thanks, Smitty.'

Ezra walked toward the hotel. The street was empty. No horses, no bicycles. Even the saloons were quiet. He passed the gentlemen's club, and he had the feeling he always had when he passed it – the feeling of being watched. He stopped and looked up at a second-story window. Yes, someone was there. He could not see him, but he knew.

Beneath the overhang of the hotel, Owen Chesterfield sat in a straight chair. His bowler was in his lap, and his bald head was visible in the darkness. He stood and walked down the steps and met Ezra in the middle of the street.

'Just where the hell have you been?'

'I thought I'd see the country in the moonlight.'

'Who's the woman?'

'You ask a lot of questions.'

'Well?'

'She's an old friend. I knew her in Missouri.'

'Stirring up old friendships isn't the best thing to do right now. You don't belong out here in the West. Your home is back East. You haven't forgotten, have you?'

'You don't let me forget.'

The electric street lamps flickered. Ezra walked past him, but Owen's question stopped him.

'Back in Missouri, did you love her?'

'Owen, you're the nosiest rascal I've ever known.'

'Well, did you?'

'Maybe I did.'

'Why didn't you marry her?'

'Because I was a fool. Letting her go was one of those mistakes I keep paying for. The debt is never settled.'

'If you get it in your head to marry her now, you'll have to take her back East.'

'I'm not sure her husband would like that.'

'Damn. You mean you've been gallivanting around the countryside with another man's wife?'

'I wasn't gallivanting.'

'You're asking to get killed.'

'I'm not worried. I have the protection of a Pinkerton.'

Ezra almost reached the steps, but again he stopped.

'Eloise knows who you are,' Owen said. 'Stokesbury does too. They figured it out.'

'Is she going to print it?'

'The newspaper is just up the street. Why don't you go ask her?'

'Did you ask her not to print it?'

'I did. Eloise Endicott likes you, maybe as much as the woman you've been wandering around with. I don't think she's going to print something to endanger you. But, Ezra, other people are going to find out who you are. You just can't keep something like that a secret forever. Some young fellow will think if he kills you, he'll be famous.'

'I guess he will. But like I said, I'm not worried. I have the protection of a Pinkerton.'

Ezra went inside the hotel. Owen ran his hand across his head.

'Damn, after all these years, I still expect hair to be up there,' he said.

He lit a cigarette and stared up the street. No lights spilled from the windows of the *Cheyenne Daily Times*. He figured Eloise Endicott had put her paper to bed. When it comes to tracking down a story, she's as good as any reporter in Chicago, he said to himself. And, for that matter, Marcus Stokesbury isn't too shabby. Stokesbury, from the *Atlanta Constitution*, was a long, long way from home. Endicott and Stokesbury had put their journalistic heads together and figured out – at least, they thought they

9

figured out – the mystery of Ezra McPherson.

I don't think she'll publish the story, Owen thought. But, then, she's a newspaperwoman. If she has a story worth printing, she may decide to print it, and soon the whole West will know that the fastest gun in the James gang is alive and well in Cheyenne, Wyoming. How many will come to try their luck against him? How many will lie in wait, beside some road, a Winchester aimed at the middle of his back?

'Ezra, you've got to go back East. You can't stay here. If you do, you'll get yourself killed.'

Andrew Swearingen leaned against the banister of the upper veranda and saw the riders. A half-dozen. They came up the long drive and disappeared into the barn. After a few minutes they emerged and went to the bunkhouse. They were serious. He knew because they did not talk. They did not laugh. Perhaps they were just tired. After all, it was late, which made him wonder what they had been doing. Rayburn would know. Later, Andrew would ask him. As foreman, Rayburn knew everything that went on at the ranch. Maybe he had sent them to lynch someone else.

He bowed his head and wanted to cry. He closed his eyes. All he could see was the young rancher swinging wildly at the end of a rope. And he saw the rancher's young brother, the hate burning in his eyes.

'If he ever has the opportunity, he will kill me,' Andrew said.

'Who's going to kill you?'

Andrew's brother, Peter, opened the door and came onto the veranda. Peter was two years older but, to Andrew, the difference in their ages seemed much greater. Peter was taller, at least a head taller. Standing next to him, Andrew felt small, and he remembered what Rose had called him in the upstairs room at the Two Rivers – 'the runt of the litter'.

'A lot of folks would probably like to. You want a cigarette?'

'Mother doesn't like you to smoke.'

'I do quite a few things she doesn't like. How is Anne?'

Andrew struck a match on the banister and lit both cigarettes. Small clouds of smoke fled into the night.

'She's uncomfortable. I'll be glad when the baby gets here. So will she.'

'She'll be OK. I know she will.'

'I'm worried, Andrew. In fact, I'm scared. If anything were to happen to her—'

'Don't talk like that,' Andrew said. 'She's strong. She'll be fine.'

'I appreciate the words of encouragement. You know, I haven't seen much of you lately.'

'I've been busy.'

'Yeah, I guess you have.'

'You've probably heard. I killed a man – in the Two Rivers.'

'Yes, I've heard.'

'He left me no choice. At least I keep telling myself that.'

'Was he going to kill you?'

'Yes. He had a pistol. He went for it. I drew faster, and now he's dead.'

'You're right. You had no choice.'

'Rayburn taught me how to use a gun. I remember the first time I shot a tin can off a fence post in the pasture. There's no telling how many bullets I used before I hit that can. Finally, when I did hit it, I thought I was really something. I wanted to make Rayburn proud. I didn't want him to think he had wasted his time on this kid from New York.

But more than that – I wanted to make Father proud. I had this idea that proving myself with a pistol would make me a man. I wanted Father to think I was a man.'

'Killing that fellow in the Two Rivers – do you think it made you a man?'

'Peter, I keep seeing that farmer lying on the floor, his whole body shaking, the blood coming out of his gut. How can something like that make anyone a man? And then the lynching. . .'

Andrew wished he had not mentioned it.

'What lynching?'

'Yesterday we strung up a young guy that Rayburn said was rustling our cattle. I wanted to stop it. I didn't think that fellow stole any of our cattle. I don't believe any jury would have convicted him of rustling, but there was nothing I could do. You believe me, don't you?'

'I have no reason not to believe you.'

'When I woke up this morning, I came out here on the veranda. It was almost as dark as it is now. There was only the faintest glow of the sun. I suddenly realized I don't know who I am. Peter, it was the strangest feeling. I thought I was becoming the man I was supposed to be.'

'You're young. You're still searching for who you are. I'd say that's normal.'

'No. I feel lost, awfully lost. I've been with a whore. Rayburn made all the arrangements. I guess that, too, was supposed to make me a man. But it's all empty. I hit her the other night. I bloodied her face. I shouldn't have done that. A man wouldn't have done that. And when I close my eyes and see that farmer on the floor and that boy swinging from the end of a rope, I know that's not who I am. People will think it is, but it's not.'

'Father knows who you are, and he's proud of you. That should be of some comfort. You see, he's not proud of me.

He thinks I'm soft, too soft to be any good in business. But I am good in business. My approach just differs from his. He came out of the war a hardened man. He has tried to build an empire here in Wyoming. Building an empire, I suppose, requires men like Rayburn – men like you, Andrew. I'm best suited for the East.'

'Peter, there's something I've never told you. You're the rock in this family. I've never told you this, Peter. I've always admired you. Sometimes I think our noble family is going to hell, but you're steady, firm. You keep the royal ship from going under. Don't worry about what Father thinks. At least you know who you are.'

Peter finished his cigarette and tossed the butt over the banister.

'Did you know that John Tisdale's brother has come to take him back East?' Peter asked.

'No.'

'You should have been at dinner yesterday. It was quite interesting. Father invited John's brother, Luke, who's staying in Cheyenne. There were these two other fellows. Marcus Stokesbury is a reporter for the *Atlanta Constitution*. Don't ask me why he's all the way out here in Wyoming. But the fellow I'm really curious about is Ezra McPherson. He's the man who stopped the train robbery. I'm sure you've heard about that. I've never met a gunfighter, unless you consider Rayburn that. But one thing is for sure – Ezra McPherson is a gunfighter. He just has that look about him. Eloise Endicott was also there. Imagine – two newspaper people at our dinner table.'

'Yeah, I guess it was interesting.'

'Well, that's not all. I think Mother and McPherson know each other.'

'What makes you think that?'

'First of all, when she came into the parlor, when she saw

him, she turned deathly pale. The way they looked at each other at the dinner table – I'm telling you they know each other. They probably knew each other in Missouri.'

Another rider galloped up the drive and headed to the barn.

'That's Mother,' Andrew said. 'She must have heard you talking about her. She's the only woman I know who wears a silk dress when she rides a horse. I wonder why she's out so late. Maybe she followed Father into town to see what he does.'

'She knows what he does. You and I know what he does. Brother, you're not the only one who visits whores, and he doesn't care about keeping it a secret. Well, I'm going to turn in.'

Peter opened the door but hesitated.

'Andrew, watch yourself.'

Near the front steps Ginevra stopped and looked up at Andrew. She did not speak. She did not lift a hand in greeting. And then she was gone.

He thought about turning in as well, but he knew he could not sleep. After ten or fifteen minutes, footsteps sounded in the upstairs hall. She wants to talk, he said to himself, and I don't want to talk to her. She came onto the veranda and stood close to him. In her hands she held a small brown leather case.

'Where've you been?' he asked.

'Riding. Sometimes I need to get away. It helps me to think.'

She held out the leather case. He smelled the newness of the leather.

'I want you to take this,' she said.

There was an urgency in her voice, and he did not understand.

'What is it?'

'It's money.'

'What have you done – robbed Father's safe?'

'I have money too. Take it. It's yours.'

'Why? I don't understand.'

'It's enough money for you to start a new life somewhere else, somewhere far from here.'

'Mother, what are you talking about? You're not making any sense.'

'I know about the lynching. You committed murder.'

Andrew froze as if a sudden burst of the northwest wind of winter had swept across the ranch and found him on the veranda. He stared at the leather case and realized his mother's hands were trembling.

'How did you find out? Who told you?'

'Never mind who told me. I know what you did. A boy has been killed, and someone has to pay. Once the sheriff starts looking into it, the trail will probably lead to you. The sheriff will come for you. The Swearingen name and the Swearingen money can protect you only so far. So you must leave. Go farther west. Go to California. I don't think the law will trail you that far.'

'Don't you think you're overreacting? From what I've heard, the sheriff is not a man willing to do much of anything. There's going to be a war between Father and the homesteaders. Haven't you heard? I doubt that Sheriff Harrison wants to be in the middle of it.'

'You're gambling that he'll do nothing. He may be pressured to do something. Andrew, you may go to prison. You may hang. Your father and that cutthroat Rayburn have led you down a path that was not meant for you. It's not too late to change, but you can't do it here. Listen to me, Andrew. Take the money and leave – tonight – while there's still time.'

'Someone has told you to tell me this.'

'It doesn't matter. But it was someone whose word I trust.'

Andrew reached out and touched the case. His fingers closed around it, and he took it. His father, Richard Swearingen, was practically a king in Wyoming. He won't let me go to prison, Andrew thought. He certainly won't let me go to the gallows. But then, perhaps Mother is right. Cheyenne isn't New York. The Swearingen money may not be enough to shield him.

'I didn't want that boy to hang,' Andrew said. 'I didn't think he rustled any of our cattle.'

'Go saddle a horse. Don't wait on the train.'

He tucked the case under his arm and left the veranda. He did not bother to go to his room and pack. Instead, he headed straight for the barn and saddled his mare. He pushed the case into his saddle bag. Before he heard a voice, he knew that someone was standing behind him.

'You seem in a rush to head somewhere.'

The voice was coarse. Rayburn came close. Andrew could not really see his face in the darkness, but he was certain the foreman was smiling.

'That's right,' Andrew said.

'You must have a hankering for Rose. Lovely Rose. She'll be glad to see you.'

'I'm through with Rose.'

'Is that a fact? I understand. She is a bit on the heavy side, but she was OK for starters. I'm sure I can fix you up with someone more to your liking.'

'No, you don't understand. I'm through with all that. I'm through with the ladies of the Two Rivers. I'm through with the killing.'

'So you're cutting out, are you? Things getting too hot for you? You just couldn't take seeing that boy swing?'

Andrew's hand went for his pistol.

'You'd better think twice before you go for that gun,' Rayburn said. 'I'm not the lovesick farmer you shot down. I don't care if you are Swearingen's kid. You go for that gun and I'll kill you.'

Andrew lowered his hand.

'I'm leaving,' Andrew said. 'Get out of my way.'

'Sure thing, kid. Your daddy gave up on your brother a long time ago. No gumption. He thought there was some hope for you. I guess he was wrong.'

'I guess he was.'

Andrew walked the mare out of the stall and out of the barn and out of the corral. He mounted and spurred her into a gallop down the drive. In the darkness of the upper veranda Ginevra stood and watched.

CHAPTER TWO

Outside the corral Curly Pike lifted the tin cup. The coffee was cold and he tossed what little remained. In the bright morning sunlight his reddish-brown beard shone more red than brown. Already beads of sweat dripped down his forehead.

'Mind if I join you?'

Wade Treutlin walked up with a plate of fried eggs, biscuits, and fatback.

'Suit yourself.'

Curly didn't consider himself a good judge of age, but he guessed that Treutlin was in his early twenties, if that old. He hadn't worked on the Swearingen ranch for long. Curly hardly knew him, so he figured he'd have to be careful what he said. Within the past few days Rayburn had hired at least a half dozen hands, and Curly suspected they knew more about guns than about cattle.

'I gotta hand it to Swearingen,' Treutlin said. 'He makes sure we have a good breakfast every morning. It ain't been that way every place I've worked.'

Treutlin pushed the sombrero back on his head.

'Sounds like you've worked a lot of places.'

'I've drifted around. No reason for me to stick around any one place too long. You see, I ain't got a home. How

18

'bout you?'

'Home is where I get paid.'

'That's me, friend. If the money runs out, I move on.'

Curly smelled smoke. It was not a pleasant smell.

'You smell like a chimney that don't draw,' Curly said. 'What have you been doing?'

'Didn't you hear? Some of us rode out last night. We had us a little bonfire.'

'What are you talking about?'

'We set fire to this homesteader's house. I think his name was Davis. It was dry tinder. Went up fast.'

'Why the hell did you do that?'

'I was told to. Just like you, I do what I'm paid to do. Swearingen pays pretty well. Forty a month. That's good money. I've never heard of a rancher who paid that kind of money.'

'Was anybody hurt?'

'Well, let me think. I'm pretty sure we hurt their feelings. Yes, sir, I'm pretty sure of that.'

'What's the point of burning someone out?'

'The next time I see Rayburn, I'll ask him. A funny thing happened when we were riding back. We came across this fellow on horseback out in the middle of nowhere. We stopped and had us a nice little chat. It turned out he was the man who shot those train robbers. McPherson's his name. I believe you brought him and some others here for dinner with the old man.'

'What of it?'

'What did you think of him?'

'He's not somebody you want to mess with.'

'If the time is right, I believe I can take him.'

'Don't be a fool.'

'Last night the time was not right. He got the jump on me. But it won't be that way in the future. I'm damn sure I can take him.'

Curly was tired of talking to the young ranch hand. Curly had looked into the dark eyes of Ezra McPherson and he didn't like what he saw. He thought about the long journey in the phaeton across the parched range. Taking McPherson, Luke Tisdale, Marcus Stokesbury, and Eloise Endicott from Cheyenne to the Swearingen ranch was not a job he wanted. He had considered telling Rayburn it was a job better left for someone else. But arguing with Rayburn was not something he cared to do.

Suddenly, as he thought about the journey in the phaeton, Curly remembered the boy swinging from a tree limb. The boy's brother had waved from a hilltop and gotten their attention. Curly didn't want to get involved, but the others insisted. In my thirty-five years on this earth, I've seen lynchings, Curly thought, but I ain't never seen someone that young at the end of a rope.

'There's talk of a range war,' Treutlin said. 'If it comes to that, I'm ready.'

Early in the morning, the ranch was busy, as busy as a small town. Riders went up and down the long drive. Curly noticed one rider didn't fit in. On the far side of the corral, Sheriff Mitch Harrison came up the drive.

'That's a fine looking sorrel,' Treutlin said. 'Who is that?'

'Sheriff Harrison.'

'What's the sheriff doing here?'

'Maybe he wants to talk to the men who burned out a homesteader last night.'

Curly, still holding the tin cup, started toward the barn.

'Curly, where you off to? What's the matter with you, Curly?'

'I'm going to do what I'm paid to do.'

*

20

The study was dark. Heavy curtains blocked the sunlight. Richard Swearingen raised his head from the mahogany desk. It was no easy task. His head throbbed and for a moment he thought he was going to vomit. His coat lay loosely across a chair near the desk. A knock at the door must have been the thing that woke him, but he wasn't sure. He rubbed his eyes. He started to lower his head, but another knock startled him.

'Yeah, who is it?'

'Peter.'

'What do you want?'

Peter opened the door and saw his father in the shadows behind the desk. The smell of liquor and stale cigar smoke sickened him.

'Sheriff Harrison is here. He wants to see you.'

'Harrison? What the hell does he want?'

'Like I said, he wants to see you.'

Swearingen pushed himself back from the desk. His head pounded even more. Peter still stood in the doorway and stared and then turned and left. His father had come in shortly before daybreak. He had tried to be quiet, but the closing of the door to the study was enough to awaken Peter.

The entrance hall outside the study was dark. Closer to the front door sunlight spilled through the fanlight.

'Damn, I dread that sunlight,' Swearingen mumbled.

He heaved his big body forward. Beyond the front door, which stood open, awaiting his arrival, the sunlight was blinding. Ginevra came into view.

'Damn, I dread that woman too.'

Sheriff Harrison sat on the sorrel, his wide-brimmed hat pulled low on his forehead to shield his eyes from the sun. He wore a brown suit, but he had shed his tie. He knew how much the mayor wanted him to wear a tie –

'We're civilized now, Sheriff,' the mayor had said – but he was not about to wear a tie during the long hot ride to Swearingen's ranch.

Swearingen's house was the biggest house the sheriff had ever seen, and he wondered why anyone would want to live in something so big. Money. It all came down to money, Harrison concluded. You've got money. You've got to spend it and show folks just how much money you've got. You've got to make a statement. You've got to intimidate.

Well, I won't be intimidated by Swearingen or anybody else, Harrison thought.

Swearingen tried to straighten himself. He left the hall and came onto the porch. He felt faint. He leaned against one of the pillars.

'Sheriff, what brings you out here so early? Old men like us need extra sleep.'

'There was some trouble yesterday, Mr Swearingen.'

'Trouble? What kind of trouble? Did one of my boys shoot up a saloon? If that's the case, I'll certainly deal with it. But you know how it is. Boys will be boys sometimes. My ranch hands work awfully hard. Sometimes they just have to blow off a little steam. Still, we can't be having that kind of stuff. I assure you, Sheriff, I'll take care of it.'

'Shooting up a saloon isn't the kind of trouble I'm talking about.'

'Well, Sheriff, just what are you talking about?'

'A lynching. I've been told your younger son, Andrew, knows something about it. I need to talk to him, but I wanted to talk to you first.'

'Well, that's kind of you, Sheriff. I don't know anything about any lynching, and I'm sure Andrew doesn't either, but we can find out. Peter, go up to your brother's room and tell him to come down here.'

'Yes, sir.'

'Sheriff, why don't you come inside and get out of the sun?'

'I'll just stay here.'

Ginevra stood not far from her husband. She did not look at him. She imagined what his appearance was. She smelled the liquor. She detected the smell of perfume, not an especially fine perfume. Well, he's in for a surprise, she thought. Andrew should be far away by now, well beyond the reach of Harrison.

Harrison shifted position in the saddle. He did not become more comfortable. Riding out to the Swearingen ranch first thing in the morning was not something he wanted to do. For one thing, he did not like Swearingen. He stared at him. The capitalist from New York, it seemed, was as big as a small Wyoming mountain. His face, red in the morning sun, was hard. The eyes were bloodshot. His white shirt was wrinkled. Harrison suspected he had been out all night. He had heard about the big man's late-night escapades.

After studying Swearingen, Harrison focused his attention on Ginevra. She was stone-faced. He had a hard time reading her thoughts, but she had a look that said she knew something that no one else knew. I'm starting to imagine things in this miserable heat, he thought. Still, something in her brown eyes conveyed that message. The sheriff then noticed Anne, Peter's wife. It was obvious the baby would come any day.

Peter walked back onto the porch.

'He's not in his room.'

'What do you mean?' Swearingen said. 'Where is he?'

'It looks like his bed hasn't been slept in. Anyway, he's not here.'

'Well, Sheriff, we have something of a problem,'

Swearingen said. 'I do not know the whereabouts of my son. I don't have to tell you. This is an awfully big ranch. He's probably out on the range somewhere. He takes a keen interest in the protection of my herd.'

'I'm sure he does.'

'I don't want to keep you from your other duties. When I find him, I'll tell him to ride into town and talk to you. I'm sure we can get everything sorted out to our satisfaction.'

'Any sorting out will be done to the satisfaction of the law.'

'Well, of course, Sheriff. That's what I meant.'

'See to it that your boy comes to see me,' Harrison said.

The sheriff headed down the drive, and Peter and Anne returned inside the house. Swearingen walked toward the barn. Riders emerged and galloped toward the western pastures.

Rayburn met him outside the barn and nodded in greeting. A cigarette hung loosely from the corner of his mouth.

'Good morning, Mr Swearingen. Did you have a nice evening in town?'

'I feel like hell this morning, so it must have been a nice evening. I guess you saw Harrison.'

'Yeah, I saw him. What'd he want?'

'He wants to speak to Andrew about what he calls a lynching. We call it something else. I don't like Harrison riding here and acting like he owns the place.'

'I don't guess you do. You want me to have a little talk with Harrison?'

'Yes, today. Now, where the hell is Andrew?'

'I don't know.'

'You're supposed to make it your business to know where everyone is.'

'Not when they decide to leave.'

'What are you talking about?'

'Andrew has left. Last night he saddled up and rode out.'

'Where was he heading?'

'He didn't say. He isn't coming back.'

'Didn't you try to stop him?'

'Me? We both know how good he is with a Colt. He was in no mood to discuss his future plans, certainly not with me.'

Swearingen did not understand. He turned and looked back at the large house. Ginevra remained on the porch. She stared at him. In the heat of the early morning he saw Ginevra and knew.

He left Rayburn and walked back to the house and stopped at the steps. Ginevra hovered above him.

'Damn you,' he said. 'What have you done?'

'I've taken care of our son, something you've been unwilling to do.'

'You know nothing about taking care of him. You've taken care of Peter and look at him.'

'I look at Peter and see a gentleman. I look at Andrew and see what you've made of him. It's not what I want. More importantly, it's not what he wants.'

'He wanted to be a man, and I've made him a man.'

'You've made him a man who has killed. He's hurting. He's lost.'

'Where is he?'

'I don't know.'

Swearingen climbed the steps more quickly than she thought possible. With the right hand he grabbed her left upper arm.

'Don't lie to me, woman.'

'I don't know. Let go!'

'I'll let go when I'm damn good and ready. What did

you say to him?'

'I told him he had to leave. I knew about the lynching. I told him Harrison would come for him.'

'There was no lynching. There was justice. How did you know about it? How are you privy to Harrison's plans?'

'It doesn't matter. What does matter is that Andrew is gone. For good.'

Swearingen released her arm and dropped onto the steps and looked at the corral, then at the barn, and then beyond.

'I've tried to build something here for my sons,' he said, 'and for their sons and for their sons. It wasn't your place to interfere, Ginevra. You had no right. You had no right.'

His voice grew weak and, for a moment, she almost pitied him. The moment was only that – a moment – and suddenly Peter came to the door.

'Mother, please hurry. It's Anne. Father, have someone go for Doc Grierson.'

Despite the heat that made the prairie a frying pan, Harrison was in no hurry to return to Cheyenne. In fact, the sorrel seemed in more of a hurry than he was.

'No rush, Josie. I've got some thinking to do.'

He thought about the letter of resignation he needed to finish writing. It lay in a desk drawer back in his office. Mayor Payne is sure going to be surprised, he said to himself, but it's time. It's past time. These old bones are creaking more than the saddle.

'You hear my bones creaking, Josie? That's right. It's my bones, not the saddle.'

Zeke Stuart is an able deputy, he thought. He'll make an able sheriff. He's young. He's got a lot to learn, but he'll be all right.

Or will he? He tends to be rash, and that can get a man

in trouble, especially a lawman. But he'll mature. Some things you just learn with age. The challenge is you have to live long enough to learn those things.

He looked to his right and to his left, at the vast prairie that stretched to the hills and to the mountains. He envisioned Swearingen's men crossing the prairie to attack the homesteaders. He envisioned the homesteaders crossing the prairie to stop them. War. Range war.

'That's what's coming.'

He had seen it before. He would be leaving Stuart right in the middle of it. Maybe he is too young for that, he thought, and I'm too old. Stuart will need help, but who's going to help him?

Once I turn in my badge, I don't want to hang around. I won't be here to help.

He thought about Penelope. She had wanted him to give up the law a long time ago.

'Let's go someplace peaceful,' she had said. 'You've given your life to the law. It's time to walk away from it.'

'I should have listened,' he said. 'Josie, I should have paid attention to what she said. I wish you had known Penelope. You would have liked her. She would have liked you. I should have taken her out of this country. She might never had got typhoid. She might still be alive today.'

He urged Josie forward. Suddenly he thought about the three strangers from the East – young Luke Tisdale, on a mission to retrieve the body of his brother. Accompanying Tisdale was Marcus Stokesbury, a reporter from the *Atlanta Constitution*.

'Josie, can you believe a reporter from the *Atlanta Constitution* is in Cheyenne? Why didn't he stay in Atlanta? You'd think there's enough news where he came from to keep him busy.'

And then there was Ezra McPherson. He had quickly

made a name for himself. He stopped a train robbery. He killed most of the robbers. He had to be Luke Tisdale's hired gun. They wanted to know who killed Tisdale's brother, John. Whoever did it was going to pay. Harrison saw it – saw the desire for vengeance in their eyes – and that desire never led to anything good. Just more killing, more quests for vengeance.

'What a trio of pilgrims. Do I want to leave that for Zeke to handle? It's one thing to handle a drunken cowpoke causing too much of a ruckus. It's something else to deal with a gunslinger like McPherson. And that's what he is, Josie, a gunslinger, pure and simple. Is Zeke ready for that?'

A rider approached in a full gallop from behind.

'Hold on, Josie. Let's see what this fellow's in such a hurry about.'

The rider drew closer.

'Well, I guess you located the young Swearingen,' Harrison said.

The barrel of the .45 shone in the sunlight. Two quick bursts from the pistol shattered the quiet of the prairie. The bullets struck Harrison in the chest and upper abdomen. He reached for the saddle horn but, instead, fell. The fall seemed, to him, to take forever. When he hit the ground, he could not feel it beneath him. His vision was blurred. He could tell that the man was still on horseback. He struggled to breathe, to find enough air to carry one word that would be no more than a whisper.

'Why?'

The man fired another shot.

CHAPTER THREE

'I did not know John Tisdale well. I wish I had known him much better. It was always a pleasure to talk to him. He was always friendly. He was always optimistic. You see, he believed in the growth of this country. He wanted to be a part of it. I know because he told me.'

The sun beat down on the cemetery. Timothy Monroe, the Methodist minister, stood, bare-headed, in a black suit. Sweat glistened on his red face and darkened his white collar. Marcus Stokesbury wondered how many funerals the minister had conducted in this cemetery. The minister was not a young man. Marcus surmised he had presided over many funerals, and many were probably for men like John Tisdale, shot down in an alley with no witnesses, only endless speculation as to who did it.

'One afternoon I was riding back to town from one of the ranches that surround Cheyenne. John was also returning to Cheyenne from the Swearingen ranch. Our paths merged and we rode together and talked. He was exuberant. "I'm going to get married," he said. "I'm going to be one of these ranchers," he said. "Oh, not one of the big ones. I'll start out small. But I want to build something and make my wife proud." He was a young man with a dream.' Monroe paused and stared first at Luke, then at Ezra.

'I had a distinct impression of John Tisdale. He was a

man who deplored violence. Still, he became caught up in it. Some of you may want vengeance. That is understandable. The murderer has never been caught. I've spoken at too many of these funerals. Violence has taken the lives of too many people lying in this cemetery, lying in the potter's field, lying on the prairie where no one came to bury them. If you're a kinsman of the gun, consider what John would want. He would want to stop the killing.'

Marcus studied Ezra. His face was hard, and Marcus wondered what he must be thinking. 'A kinsman of the gun . . .' Marcus let the words seep into his memory. One day, hopefully soon, he would return to the newspaper in Atlanta and sit at his desk and feel the impatient eyes of his editor fixed upon him and he would write the article about Ezra McPherson. He would remember the minister's words. Someday he would ask Ezra what he thought about them. Did he consider himself 'a kinsman of the gun'? He knew what Ezra's reply would be, and it would be no reply at all.

Then Marcus turned his attention to the men and women who had come. Beside him was Eloise Endicott, a fellow journalist, publisher of the Cheyenne newspaper. She wore a long dark blue dress and matching hat with a wide brim. Jennifer Beauchamp, the schoolteacher from South Carolina who had come West to start a new life, stood next to Luke. The young doctor's eyes remained fixed on the open hole in the earth. On the other side of Luke stood his friend, Ezra McPherson, and Owen Chesterfield, a Pinkerton. All the men held their hats in their hands. Meta Anderson was there, along with a man and woman that Marcus figured were her parents. When the minister spoke of the woman John Tisdale intended to marry, Marcus knew he spoke of Meta. She and her parents were dressed simply. Life for them on the Wyoming prairie,

Marcus imagined, was hard, too hard to be able to afford anything that came close to fine clothes. Zeke Stuart, the deputy's badge bright in the sun, was there, and Marcus wondered why. The Swearingens were absent. Marcus had expected them to come.

The monuments in the cemetery were both plain and ornamental, and Marcus thought about Oakland Cemetery back in Atlanta. It was a place to escape to. You could wander among the trees and monuments and think. You could look at the tombstones and see the history of Atlanta that stretched back before the war. You could look at the city cemetery of Cheyenne and see that history taking shape.

'Luke Tisdale, John's brother, wants to say a few words,' Timothy Monroe said.

Jennifer touched Luke's hand, only for a moment.

'John liked to encourage people,' Luke said. 'If people were ever down, he tried to lift them up. Sometimes I didn't know whether I would get through medical college, but John encouraged me. He kept me going. He was a brother. He was a friend. John, I'm going to miss you.'

Luke wanted to say more, but he decided that was enough. He stepped back to Jennifer. He didn't remember much of what the minister said. He remembered 'ashes to ashes, dust to dust,' but that was about all. And then the service was over.

He saw Meta, and he thought he should say something to her. John would want him to.

'I'm glad you came,' Luke said. 'Are these your parents?'

'Yes,' Meta said.

'I'm sorry for your loss,' the father said. 'Meta, we've got to get back.'

'I'll come directly.'

31

Meta held purple New England aster. It was a flower John liked. He liked the name, especially the New England part. 'New England in Wyoming,' he would say. 'Two worlds I love.' She walked to the grave and looked down at the plain pine box. She could not believe that a box could hold someone like John. His dreams were too big to be contained in such a box. She looked up and saw Eloise. Her dress was beautiful. Meta felt shabby and ashamed. She should have worn something special for John, but she had nothing special and as long as she lived on the desolate prairie, she would have nothing. John had helped her dream of possibilities, but he was gone and so was the dream.

Eloise walked to her and for a while neither spoke. The sun lit up the aster, and Meta kneeled and tossed the flowers onto the coffin.

'They're beautiful,' Eloise said.

'I have to go. Ma and Pa are waiting.'

Meta walked to the wagon where her parents sat. Her father fidgeted with the reins.

'She loved him,' Eloise said.

'Yes, I think she did,' Luke said.

Ezra laid a hand, strong and sun-darkened, on his shoulder.

'Ezra, I wish I could find who did this,' Luke said.

'Whoever did this is a coldblooded killer,' Ezra said. 'Killing comes easy to him.'

'In other words, I'm not the kind of man to go after such a killer.'

'No, Luke, you're not.'

Ezra put his black hat on, and he and Owen headed for the gate. Stuart stood by himself.

'Deputy, you look lost,' Owen said.

'I didn't know John Tisdale. I just thought I should

come. Don't ask me why. I just did.'

'Well, that's mighty kind of you.'

'Deputy, something's troubling you,' Ezra said. 'No point in telling me there's not. What is it?'

'The sheriff.'

'What about the sheriff?' Owen asked.

'He rode out to the Swearingen place early this morning. He wanted to talk to Andrew Swearingen about the lynching. He should be back by now.'

'Maybe he stopped at a friend's place to have a cup of coffee,' Owen said.

'No, I don't think so. I don't guess I should be bothering you about this, especially right after a funeral. We didn't exactly make you feel welcome when you got to Cheyenne. I'm worried.'

'Let's saddle up,' Ezra said. 'We'll go with you. Owen, we'll get horses at the livery.'

Marcus and Eloise walked with the minister out of the cemetery. The gravediggers slouched outside the gate, near the black hearse with two large windows on each side. They grinned at Marcus. He thought that if a buzzard could grin, it would look something like that.

Luke and Jennifer were alone. She took his hand, and he wanted to tell her how much he appreciated her being there. He looked into her eyes, and he knew it wasn't necessary. They left the grave, and the New England aster glowed on the lid of the coffin.

The old man sat, cross-legged, next to the small campfire, a sweat-stained flop hat on the ground at his side. Already the sun burned the eastern sky. Behind him flowed a stream, shallow but swift. In his lap he held a Sharps. It was cocked. He kept a finger on the trigger. A black patch covered his left eye. With his good eye he focused on the rider who had come into his camp.

'Nice looking mare you're riding, sonny,' the old man said.

'She gives me no reason to complain.'

'Then she's a whole heap better'n most people.'

'I just need to water me and my horse.'

'Help yourself. It don't belong to me. I'm simply passing through, same as you, I figger.'

Andrew led the mare to the stream. He kneeled and cupped his hands and drank. The water was cold. Amazing, he thought, in this heat. He drank again and stood.

'I see you looking at my coffee pot,' the old man said. 'Now that you've had some water, sit a spell. Pour yourself a cup of coffee.'

'I'm obliged.'

The old man pulled a tin cup from the saddle-bags next to him and tossed it. Andrew poured, then sat and waited for the coffee to cool. He stared across the prairie. In the distance vast rocky peaks stood guard in the west.

'You've been doing some riding,' the old man said.

Andrew nodded.

'Let me guess. You were calling on a young lady, but then her husband came home early, or maybe, even worse, it was her daddy, and so you had to make a hasty getaway.'

'Nowhere close. This heat is playing tricks with your imagination.'

'Where you coming from?'

'Cheyenne.'

'Ain't been there. I hear tell there's a lot of money there.'

'I guess.'

'Well, I wish money could solve the world's problems, but it never has and never will. Of course, if somebody wants to give me money, I ain't gonna turn it down.'

The old man laughed and then coughed.

'It has to be lonely out here all by yourself,' Andrew said.

'I've got my horse and I've got my mule. I ain't lonely. You can always talk to a horse and a mule, and they ain't gonna argue back. Tell me, sonny. What are you running from?'

'What makes you think I'm running from something?'

'I'm a pretty good judge of people. I can tell when they're trying to get away from something, and I can tell when they're in a hurry to do it.'

You're a nosy old man, Andrew thought, and he wanted to tell him, but the rifle made him reconsider. Red splotches dotted the old man's face above his white beard.

'I see you're taking an interest in this rifle,' the man said. 'It's a Sharps, 1874. I've knocked down many a buffalo with it. Had to keep the railroad men's stomachs full. Also needed to draw a paycheck when the prospectin' warn't going good.'

The old man wore buckskin. His horse and pack mule stood, hobbled, beside the stream. A shovel and pick, tied on the mule, caught Andrew's attention.

'How long you been a prospector?'

'Since Dahlonega. Ever heard of it?'

'Can't say I have.'

'Down in Georgia. Big gold strike there a long time ago. I took a Cherokee wife when I was there. Finest woman the sun ever shined on. Her and me left the north Georgia mountains with her people. The government said they had to go West. She didn't make it. I held her in my arms when she died.'

'I'm sorry.'

'We have to go on, sonny. I kept going West. To California. One of these days I'm gonna strike it rich. I thought I'd head up into the Black Hills. I hear tell there's still some nuggets up there. I may find a few.'

'What happened to your eye?'

'A Comanche took a liking to it in Texas before the war.'

Andrew wondered how far he had ridden. He wondered where he was. Surely he was out of Wyoming.

'What's your name, sonny?'

'Andrew.'

'If I had any friends, they'd call me Phil.'

The old man's voice was raspy. It was as if he dragged his words across sandpaper. His white hair was thin on top and long in the back. His beard had not seen shears in many months. He wore dark brown moccasins.

'Them two biscuits and salt pork in the skillet are yours if you want 'em.'

'They would go good with the coffee. Thanks, mister.'

'You know, there's nothing like a good cup of coffee to get the day off to an acceptable start.'

Andrew ate quickly. Biscuits had never tasted so good. He finished the coffee. He looked at the mountains. Tall, rugged. They almost touched the sky. Beyond the mountains he would be safe. He would settle in California. That's what his mother wanted. It was a good idea. He had enough money to buy a small ranch. The only problem was that he really didn't know anything about ranching. That was one thing Rayburn hadn't taught him.

'I need to be moving on,' he said.

'You know, sonny, running isn't going to take care of the problem. It's always going to be there. You think you can escape it, but you can't. You'll wake up in the middle of the night in a cold sweat. You'll think you've heard something. You'll think they've found you. You'll reach for your Colt and you'll realize your hand is shaking. You wouldn't be able to hit anything if you pulled the trigger. You'll try to go back to sleep. You'll close your eyes. But if you've killed a man, you'll see his face. You'll see the blood around the hole where your bullet took him down. And you know what? You'll cry – like a baby. You'll keep running, but the past will haunt you. You'd better realize it now. You've got to stand up and face it. Running ain't going to do any good.'

Andrew stood and went again to the stream and bent and cupped his hands and splashed water into his face.

'I'm just an old man. You don't have to believe a word I've said.'

At night Andrew had closed his eyes and had seen the farmer on the floor of the saloon, the dark blood pooling around his quaking body. Again he reached into the stream and drank. Then he went to his horse.

'No need to rush off,' the old man said. 'Talking is the only thing I'm good at.'

'Mister, I appreciate your hospitality. I hope you find the gold you're looking for.'

'I hope so too. I don't think you're looking for gold. Whatever it is you're looking for, I hope you find it.'

Andrew took one last look at the mountains. Beyond the peaks he would be safe. No one would find him. Money could give him a new life. He looked at the cold stream. He looked at the old man, who lifted a hand in farewell, and then he spurred his horse back toward the east. He did not go far. He figured he should pay something for the coffee and food. The old geezer looked like he was broke. He reined his horse in to return.

The old man was gone.

Long before Curly reached the blackened ruins, the smoke stung his nostrils. He got down from his horse and stood close to the chimney. A monument of defiance, it had refused to collapse. At his feet lay a ragdoll with red hair.

The face was smudged.

He squatted next to the charred wood and stared. Rayburn would wonder where he was. That was OK, he said to himself. Let him wonder. He stood and walked the circumference of the ruins. He didn't know why he did it. It was as if he was expecting to find something, but there was nothing to find. There was nothing left of the dream that brought these homesteaders to Wyoming.

He didn't hear the horse approach until it was almost upon him. He rose quickly, his hand on his revolver. He expected to find Rayburn, maybe Treutlin. He expected trouble.

'Andrew, what are you doing?'

'I don't know. I really don't know. I've just been wandering. Somehow this is where I've ended up. What are you doing here? Whose place was this?'

'The Davis family. I didn't know them. Some of your pa's men burned them out last night. I'm like you. I don't know why I came here. It seems like I've been here for hours.'

Andrew reached for the canteen tied to the saddle horn. He offered it to Curly. First Curly drank, then Andrew.

'I reckon they came here looking for a new start,' Andrew said. 'I'm sure they didn't expect this.'

Curly stared at him. Andrew's face was a dark red. His eyes had some sort of glaze.

'Are you all right? Do you need to see Doc Grierson?'

'Why do you ask?'

'You talk as if you actually care what happened to this family.'

A gust of wind came out of the north and carried the smoke higher. It swirled against the blue sky and vanished. Andrew dismounted and walked to the ruins. He ran the toe of his boot through the ash.

'Curly, do you ever think about how things have turned

out in your life?'

'Can't say I do. What'd be the point? You ain't old enough to be asking questions like that. Those are questions for old men that haven't got much time left on their clocks. Have you been drinking something besides water? You ain't gotten into dope, have you? Man, if you've gotten into dope, your old man is gonna be fit to be tied.'

'No, I haven't gotten into dope.'

'I hear tell Rose has gotten into it. You got a hankering for Rose? I bet she misses you something terrible.'

'Curly, I've been running. At least trying to run.'

'What are you running from?'

'I could have stopped something bad from happening, and I didn't. Far to the west of here I met this old man—'

'What old man?'

'He said he was a gold prospector. He had a Sharps. It was a fine looking rifle. For a moment I thought he was going to shoot me with it. Instead, we talked. He was a strange old man. And then he was gone.'

'Andrew, you've been in this sun too long. It's addled your brain, not that you have much of one.'

'I'm supposed to be your boss. You're not supposed to talk to your boss like that.'

'You're the boss, son. That's not the same. Besides, your old man ain't my boss no more.'

'You've quit?'

'I'm not working for him anymore,' Curly said, and he stared at the lonesome chimney. 'Not after this. I haven't told him. I don't like the way things are heading. I ain't going back to your pa's ranch and when I don't go back, I reckon he can figure things out.'

'You remember that farmer I shot in the Two Rivers?'

'I ain't likely to forget.'

'I can't get him out of my mind. I had convinced myself

I was a hotshot with a gun. I knew I could never be like Peter. He's brilliant with numbers. He knows more about finance than Father does, even though Father will never admit it. For some reason, Father doesn't think Peter is much of a man. Father was at Gettysburg. Did you know that?'

'No, I didn't.'

'He was. He has talked about Pickett's charge, about the men that died in the open field. Father sent many a Reb to meet his maker. Somehow I think he has the idea that, to be a man, you've got to prove yourself with a gun. Maybe the war gave him that idea. I guess I proved something with a gun. At least that's the way Father looks at it.'

'You proved you can take care of yourself.'

'I shouldn't have been there in the first place.'

'It's over with. Everyone knows it was self-defense.'

Andrew picked up the doll and went back to his horse.

'Just where do you think you're going?'

'Wherever these wagon tracks lead. This doll belongs to somebody. I want to make sure she gets it back.'

'It looks like the tracks lead to the Anderson place. If I was you – and I sure am glad I'm not – I don't think I'd set foot on their spread. When they find out who you are—'

'You said I can handle myself. I'm not worried.'

'You should be.'

Andrew followed the tracks of the wagon wheels. Curly shook his head and mounted.

'I'm coming too. Maybe I can keep them from filling you full of holes.'

CHAPTER FOUR

Jeremy Anderson and Lem Davis stood in the yard in front of the porch and surveyed the late afternoon sunburned sky the way farmers do when they look for any sign of rain. They did not have to look hard. No clouds. A steady wind might blow some rain their way, but no wind stirred. Anderson still wore the black suit, dust-covered from the trip into Cheyenne. It was his only suit, and he didn't like wearing it.

'I hate imposing on you like this,' Davis said. 'I had no idea you were in town for a funeral. I bet you were surprised to return and find us here.'

'You're more than welcome to stay as long as you want,' Anderson said.

'We won't stay long. I've decided to take the family back to Ohio.'

The acrid smell of smoke still clung to Davis. His shoulders sagged. Normally he would have stood taller than Anderson, but not today. He had not reached forty, but he looked much older. His wife, Victoria, looked even older. Their life had been hard, and he blamed himself. He shouldn't have made her come West. She said there was nothing wrong with the land in Ohio, but he thought there was something better in Wyoming. She wouldn't say it, but she was bitter. He knew it.

And then there was little Caroline. He would never forget her face when the flames devoured their home, when the flames, orange-red and menacing, wrapped around the chimney that refused to collapse. She did not cry. She simply stared, a vacant look in her small green eyes. He wanted to protect their home, but there was nothing he could do. He could not go up against Swearingen's men without getting killed. Getting killed would not help his wife and daughter.

'Are you sure that's the best thing to do?' Anderson asked.

'Right now it seems like the only thing to do.'

'You can build back. I'll help. I've got three strong sons. They'll help. And there's plenty of neighbors. They'll all help. That's what neighbors do.'

'Those men who burned us out – they said if they ever found us on our place again, they'd kill us. I believe them.'

'Lem, we've got to stand our ground. This land is our land. We can't let them push us off.'

'Victoria doesn't like it out here. She never wanted to come in the first place. Now she's scared. And little Caroline. I don't want her to go through something like that again.'

Far down the narrow dusty road two riders appeared. At first Davis and Anderson thought their eyes might be fooling them. Who would be calling so late in the afternoon? They grew nervous.

'Looks like we have more company,' Anderson said.

'I don't recognize them. They don't look like homesteaders.'

'I'm going to get my rifle.'

'Do you have an extra one?'

'I've got a Remington pistol. You and me and my three

boys ought to be enough to run them off if they try to cause any trouble.'

Anderson went inside the cabin and, followed by his sons, soon returned and handed a shotgun to Davis.

'I keep the pistol in the dresser, but it ain't there. I can't believe it just got up and walked off. My wife keeps telling me I'm getting forgetful. Maybe I took it to the barn and left it there. But this shotgun will get the job done.'

The riders drew closer. The sons, Asa and Cash and Alex Anderson, held their rifles tightly, and their father sensed the tension.

'These men may not mean any harm,' Anderson said. 'So don't start shooting unless it's called for. But, just in case, spread out. If they try anything, we'll make it hard on them.'

The riders stopped near the front steps.

'I'm looking for Mr Davis,' Andrew said.

He held the doll. Suddenly a young girl cried.

'Caroline, come back here!' a woman shrieked.

Her mother, panic on her leather-lined, weather-beaten face, reached for her, but she jumped down the steps.

'Millie! You found Millie!'

Andrew lowered the doll and the young girl took it and held it close. He had never seen a face that looked so happy.

'Mister, I don't know who you are,' Davis said, 'but that's a kind thing you've done.'

'Are you Davis?'

'Indeed I am.'

'I'm sorry you had trouble,' Andrew said.

He removed the leather satchel his mother had given him and tossed it at Davis's feet.

'What's that?' Davis asked.

'It'll pay for lumber, for essentials.'

'I've decided to take my family back East.'

'Don't let people run you off your land,' Andrew said. 'Stay and build something.'

'Who are you?' Anderson asked.

'Andrew Swearingen. This is Curly Pike.'

'Swearingen. Why, you're the man who killed Sven Burleson in the Two Rivers. And it was your father's men—'

'We don't want any trouble,' Curly said. 'That's not why we came here. We'll move on.'

'No, wait,' Anderson said. 'This is the damnedest thing. I feel like I oughtta kill both of you, but something's telling me not to. Have you eaten? The womenfolk are rustling up some food.'

'You would let a Swearingen enter your home?'

'Today I would. I don't plan to make a habit of it though.'

Andrew and Curly went inside the small cabin and removed their hats. The windows were small and the room was almost as dark as if it were night. A kerosene lamp burned dimly in the middle of a rough-hewn pine table. The young girl sat on the floor and hugged her doll. Meta Anderson stood at the dry sink beside her mother and Davis's wife. She stared at Andrew.

'John Tisdale worked for you,' she said.

'He worked for my father.'

'We've just come back from his funeral,' she said.

'John Tisdale was a good man,' Curly said. 'It's hard – it's hard to see a man like that get killed.'

'You know who killed him, don't you? Mr Swearingen, it was your foreman, Rayburn, wasn't it?'

'Meta, that's enough questions,' her father said. 'I've asked these men to have supper.'

Meta walked past Andrew and out the door.

'She took John Tisdale's death awfully hard,' her mother said.

Davis handed the leather satchel to his wife. She opened it.

'Where did all this money come from?'

'It looks like we're ranchers once again.'

'Silas Taylor has a sawmill and lumber yard in back of his general store,' Andrew said. 'You'll find all that you need there.'

Andrew thought that Davis's wife would look pleased, but she didn't. If anything, her face conveyed disappointment, resignation.

After finishing cornbread crumbled into glasses of buttermilk, Andrew and Curly drank coffee.

'I guess you boys know there's going to be a range war,' Anderson said. 'Men like your pa don't want to share the range with folks like us. We've bought our land fair and square. We have a right to it, but some men just don't look at it that way.'

'Your old man wants a war,' Davis said. 'No two ways about it – that's what he wants.'

'The lynching of that Darton boy set the wheels of war into motion, and now Davis getting burned out—'

'What if someone pays for what happened to the Darton boy?' Andrew asked.

'What do you mean?' Anderson said.

Curly set his coffee cup down on the table. The cup came down hard, harder than he intended.

'What are you talking about?' Curly said.

'What if someone steps forward and accepts punishment for what happened? Will that prevent a war?'

'Maybe, for now. I can't say for sure,' Anderson said. 'I think a war is inevitable. It might be put off for a brief spell. Who knows? But it's coming. No two ways about it.'

'It's getting late. Come on, Curly. Thank you for your hospitality. You're good people.'

'Mister, you're planning to do something,' Davis said. 'Just what is it?'

Andrew did not answer. He and Curly went outside and climbed into their saddles. Only then did Andrew notice that Meta Anderson stood in the lengthening shadows of the low-slung porch. Her stare froze him.

'John was a good lawyer,' she said. 'Your father wanted him to manipulate the law. He wasn't content with the thousands of acres he already owned. He wanted more, and he wanted John to use the law to help him get more. It didn't matter if people got hurt, if people lost every penny they had. When John wouldn't do it, when he wouldn't follow orders, your father had him killed. You know exactly what happened. Rayburn pulled the trigger as sure as you're sitting on that horse. I don't expect you to admit it. Tell Rayburn he's not going to get away with it.'

'I don't plan to have any more conversations with Rayburn,' Andrew said.

'Ma'am, let the law handle this thing,' Curly said.

'The law has had plenty of time to handle this thing. The law has done nothing.'

'Come on, Andrew,' Curly said.

Meta stood on the porch long after the riders disappeared into the twilight. The western sky was red. John always liked this time of day. She had heard him say it many times.

'One of these days I'm going to build a cabin – a log cabin – on this big prairie,' he said. 'It's going to have a front porch and in the evening you and I are going to sit in rocking chairs on the front porch and watch the sun drop into the fire of the western sky. We'll do that every evening

– well, maybe not in the winter. I've heard it gets pretty cold out here. But we'll grow old in that cabin, with lots of children and grandchildren.'

'John Tisdale, you ain't a rancher. What are you going to do with a ranch?'

'I'm going to make a home, Meta. A home for you and me. And we're going to sit on the porch and watch the fire in the sky. Of course, if any of our neighbors need a little legal help, well, I am a lawyer. I'll find time to help them.'

She listened. She heard his words again.

I hear you, John, she said to herself. I'm on the porch. But, John, I'm alone. I'm so alone. I don't think I'll ever feel any different. Not all the memories in the world are going to change that.

Shopkeepers finished counting the money in their registers and were ready to go home. Twilight settled on Cheyenne. They were eager to escape the heat of their stores. They went outside, closed the doors behind them, and turned the locks. They did not expect to see the riders coming slowly down the street.

'Who's that with Zeke Stuart?' one asked.

'Damned if I know.'

'No, wait – it's that McPherson fellow and one of his friends.'

'They're bringing someone back.'

'Who is it?'

'No, I don't believe it.'

'Who is it?'

'Oh, damn, it's the sheriff. He's the one tied across the saddle.'

Benjamin Payne examined his accounts ledger on top of the counter in his haberdashery. He could not see the figures well in the dim light, but he was pleased. Business was good. He did not need to read the figures. It was interesting how one thing led to another. Success in business had led to success in politics. He never planned to run for mayor. It was not something he had prepared for, but things had just worked out. And Cheyenne was booming.

He sensed a movement outside. He heard the voices of his fellow shopkeepers. Something was going on. He left the counter and stepped onto the sidewalk. Riders moved slowly down the street. One of the horses bore a terrible burden.

The riders stopped in front of the sheriff's office. Stuart's eyes were red. He could not see clearly. Tears mixed with the dust, and he rubbed his eyes and looked at the front of the jail building. Never again would he see Harrison walk through the door. Why – why would anyone want to kill him? He remembered what the minister had said at John Tisdale's funeral. He had spoken at many funerals. Violence had taken many lives.

Silas Taylor came out of his general store and saw the crowd that gathered around the horsemen. He walked toward them. Suddenly the mayor was by his side, breathing heavily.

'I can't believe something like this has happened,' Benjamin Payne said. 'Poor old Mitch. Can you imagine what it's going to do to our image? And to business? This is not what this town needs.'

'It's not what the sheriff needed.'

'That's what I meant.'

Silas walked faster and left the mayor behind. By the time he reached the group of bystanders, Timothy Monroe, bareheaded, stood next to Stuart.

'Son, come inside the jail.'

'That's right,' Ezra said. 'Listen to the preacher. Owen, you stay with him. I'll take care of the sheriff.'

Marcus and Eloise stood on the sidewalk outside the newspaper office. The curious spilled out of the stores and rushed toward the jail. Marcus started to go also, but then Ezra headed away, leading the horse with Harrison to Slade's. He did not see Marcus or Eloise. At least, if he did, he did not acknowledge it. The twilight grew darker, and Eloise felt a chill. A chill in this heat, she thought.

Lawrence Byrd, the sleeves of his white shirt rolled up past his elbows, walked out of the office. He looked up the street.

'Who got killed?'

'Sheriff Harrison.'

'I'm – I'm stunned. Who would have expected—'

'Nobody ever expects something like this. I want you to go to the jail. Zeke Stuart is in there. Find out what happened. We'll have to replate the front page.'

'Yes, ma'am.'

'And after you write the story, get on the telegraph. The papers in New York will want to know about this.'

'Sure thing.'

He went back inside the office and soon emerged, a notepad and pencil in his hand. He ran toward the jail. Eloise did not watch. Instead, her eyes followed Ezra. He was at Slade's now. He was still sitting in his saddle, in the darkness.

CHAPTER FIVE

Into the blackness of the night, some of the ranch hands drifted out of the bunk house and lit cigarettes. They were tired of poker. They were tired of the heat. The open air gave them relief from the poker, but not from the heat. They looked at the big house and saw Swearingen, a silhouette next to one of the columns.

'Stringbean, I bet the boss ain't too happy with you,' one said. 'He gave you a job to do, and you failed.'

'Hell, it warn't my fault Doc Grierson was out of town somewheres. I was sent to fetch him, but fetchin' warn't possible.'

'Is that why Peter Swearingen headed out later?'

'Reckon so. I heard tell he went to git the other doctor – Tisdale, John Tisdale's brother.'

'I guess he figured if he got something done right, he had to do it himself. Stringbean, we're sorely disappointed in you.'

'Yeah, Stringbean, you make us look bad.'

'To hell you say,' Stringbean said. 'You look bad and it ain't none of my doin'. Fact is – you were born lookin' bad.'

'No need to hurt my feelings.'

Their cigarettes burned red in the darkness of the

Wyoming night. They shuffled their feet and glanced at the big man still on the veranda, still leaning against the column as if he could do a better job of support than it could.

'Has anybody seen Curly Pike?' one asked.

'Not since this morning. He rode out and hasn't been back.'

'I wonder if he quit.'

'If he don't come back, I'd say he quit.'

'That's right smart of you, Stringbean. The way you figure things out, you should be in one of them Eastern schools.'

'I've thought about it.'

'Well, keep thinking.'

'I wonder why Harrison was here this morning,' the tallest of the group said.

'I couldn't hear what was said,' one of the men said, 'but I don't think it was a social call. Nobody looked too pleased. The old man looked like he was half dead. Must have had quite a night in town.'

'He's had quite a few of those lately.'

'But why do you think Harrison rode out here?'

'I bet it had something to do with Andrew.'

'Where is that young scoundrel anyway?'

'Haven't you heard?'

'No.'

'He cleared out.'

'What do you mean?'

'He's gone. I've heard he ain't coming back.'

'He left his old man?' Stringbean asked.

'That's right.'

'So, both Andrew and Curly Pike are gone.'

'Looks like it.'

'Maybe Harrison was looking for Andrew. Maybe he

knew Harrison would come for him, and so he cleared out.'

'Why would Harrison come for him? I heard he shot that farmer fair and square, pure self-defense.'

'I ain't talking about that farmer.'

'Then what the hell are you talking about?'

'The lynching.'

'What lynching?'

'Where have you been? One of the homesteaders got lynched. He was nothing but a boy. At least that's what I heard. Rayburn was in on it. Said the boy was rustling Swearingen cattle. Andrew was part of it too.'

'Then it makes sense Harrison would come out here.'

'I bet the old man wasn't happy.'

'I've never seen him happy.'

'He'll do what he has to to protect Andrew.'

'None of this sounds good. I don't like what's going on. I keep hearing talk of a range war.'

'It's just talk.'

'Have you ever been in a range war?'

'No.'

'Well, I have. Just the talk of one makes me a mite uncomfortable.'

Treutlin walked out of the bunk house. 'What makes you a mite uncomfortable?' he asked.

'Talk of a range war.'

'Nothing to worry about,' Treutlin said. 'If the bullets start flying, just stand behind me. I'll protect you.'

Treutlin laughed and walked away.

'I don't like that guy.'

'Me neither. He's supposed to be good with a gun.'

'Reckon that's why Rayburn hired him.'

Richard Swearingen stared at the ranch hands and wondered what they were talking bout. A sudden shriek came from one of the upstairs bedrooms. Anne was having a hard time of it. He wished Peter would hurry back with Luke Tisdale. He did not like the sounds he was hearing.

He thought about Andrew. He wondered where he was. Probably a long way from Cheyenne by now. Probably some place where the law would not find him.

There was no need for him to run, Swearingen thought. I would not have let anything happen to him. Running makes him look guilty. It was not Ginevra's concern. She should not have meddled in something that was none of her business.

He looked toward the east, then toward the west. One day it was going to be Andrew's. That was his plan. Peter was good with numbers. He belonged in New York. Andrew belonged in Wyoming.

'I hope you're OK, boy.'

Silas Taylor rocked back and forth in front of the dormant fireplace and smoked his pipe. Across from him Luke sat on the sofa and listened. Jennifer sang to her son in the bedroom. Her voice was soft, and he didn't think he had ever heard anything quite so lovely. He imagined her running her fingers through Bobby's hair. He realized Silas was observing him.

'Yes, she has a nice voice,' Silas said. 'I don't imagine it'll be too long before Bobby is asleep. In fact, it won't be too long before I'm asleep.'

'I hope I'm not keeping you and Mrs Taylor up. I hope my coming around isn't an imposition.'

'Not at all. You being a doctor raises the chance of intellectual conversation.'

'I heard that,' Charlotte said from the kitchen. 'As if you don't get intellectual conversation from me.'

'Damn – that woman hears everything. I'd better go in

there and help with the dishes.'

Jennifer came out of the bedroom and Luke stood.

'Let's go on the porch,' she said.

They sat in the swing and listened to the stillness of the night. He touched her hand and felt the warmth.

'It was kind of you to come to the cemetery. I appreciate it.'

'There's no need to thank me.'

'I wish you had known John,' he said. 'You would have liked him.'

'I'm sure I would have. I felt so sorry for Meta Anderson. It's obvious she felt deeply about your brother.'

'I think he cared deeply about her.'

'What are you going to do now? Are you going back East?'

He looked at her. Leaving was the last thing he wanted to do. As long as she was in Cheyenne, he wanted to stay. He wondered whether she knew.

'I – I don't know.'

'Maybe you should stay in Cheyenne. Of course, it would be hard not to go back to Boston. I'm sure you have many friends and many patients in Boston.'

'Boston has wonderful people.'

'And probably many doctors.'

'Yes, many.'

'Cheyenne has only one.'

'Do you think Cheyenne needs more doctors?'

'It's not important what I think.'

'Of course it is,' he said. 'I've talked with Doctor Grierson. He's not averse to the idea. But it's more complicated than that.'

'How so?'

'There's Ezra.'

'I don't understand.'

'Ezra came with me to make sure I didn't get into any sort of trouble. If I stay, he may get it in his head to stay too.'

'So?'

'He can't stay. He has to go back.'

'But why?'

'He just does. There are some things I can't explain.'

'Luke, what happened to Sheriff Harrison – Silas told me – no matter what you do or don't do, your friend may feel compelled to stay, to help. I'll never forget what your friend did after that train robber struck Bobby. There's just something about him that tells me he wants to help people who need help, and the people in this town and on the farms need help. It's the same with you. You're a doctor, and you want to help people.'

'Ezra helps people in different ways.'

'I know little about this sort of thing, but I feel the new sheriff will need the kind of help Ezra can provide.'

She's right, Luke thought. If Zeke Stuart becomes the sheriff, he will need help. Ezra has a special gift, a special gift with a Colt .45. But he won't do anything unless Stuart asks.

'Tell me – how are things coming along at the school?'

'Wonderfully. I'm getting the classroom ready. There are three other teachers, young ladies, and they've been eager to help. I think I'm really going to like it here.'

'I'm sure the school will consider itself lucky to have you.'

'You don't know anything about my teaching ability.'

'Oh, I can sense things like that.'

'You can, can you? I'm impressed. Can you sense what I'm thinking?'

'Yes.'

'What am I thinking?'

'You're thinking when is he going to stop talking and kiss me?'

He leaned toward her but stopped. A rider hurried to the fence gate and tied his horse. He ran to the foot of the porch steps.

'Doctor Tisdale, thank God I've found you. Smitty told me you might be here.'

'Peter, what's wrong?'

'It's my wife. The baby. Doctor Grierson is out of town. My wife. We need help. Please.'

Luke stood.

'I'll get my bag. It's at the hotel.'

'I'm coming with you,' Jennifer said. 'Don't look so surprised. I know something about having a baby.'

CHAPTER SIX

Two of the Cheyenne city council members stood in the dim light of the sheriff's office. Two sat in straight chairs. One stood close to the brass spittoon that sat on the floor at the edge of the desk. Eloise Endicott tried to remember a time when she had seen so many glum faces. A single light bulb hung from the ceiling, and a small lamp on the desk cast a yellow glow. The councilmen looked as if they faced a big problem, and they had no idea how to solve it. Mayor Payne stood in front of Harrison's desk and faced the councilmen. He tried to impart confidence, to give the impression that things, while they looked bad, would be all right. Somehow, Eloise observed, his efforts were missing the mark. He was supposed to be their leader. She figured that if she were to ask the councilmen, they would express little confidence in Payne's ability to solve the problem.

Off to the side, near Eloise, stood Ezra, Marcus, and Owen. Payne had asked Ezra and Owen to be at the meeting. Eloise had heard him and she had heard the replies.

'I don't see any point in my being there,' Ezra had said.

'Nor do I,' Owen had said. 'Mayor, I appreciate you asking us, but it's not really our affair.'

'But it is, gentlemen. Mr McPherson, you stopped a

57

train robbery not far from here. Both of you went with Zeke to find the sheriff. Whether you like it or not, whether you realize it, you've become involved in what happens here.'

Marcus stood next to Eloise. She knew he wanted to be there. A story was developing, and, like her, he wanted to be right in the middle. The two councilmen who stood kept shifting their feet. They were shopkeepers. They knew nothing of range wars and murder.

Stuart sat in a straight chair next to the wall. He could not sit in the swivel chair. It was Harrison's. As far as Stuart was concerned, no one else could occupy it. He did not think he was man enough to occupy it. Suddenly he felt like a boy. For a moment he wished he was back on his family's farm. By now the cows would be milked. His ma and pa and brothers and sisters who were still at home would be sitting and sewing and talking. They would not be talking about murder.

Payne considered what to say. He never thought something like this would happen. He was a haberdasher. To the citizens of Cheyenne, he thought, he represented business. And this meeting had a lot to do with business. Without a sheriff, the town was vulnerable, which was bad for business. If companies considering a move to Cheyenne perceived that the town had fallen back into violence, they would look elsewhere. Customers would hesitate to shop. He had suggested to Harrison numerous times that more deputies should be hired. Harrison insisted that he and Stuart would be enough to deal with any problems. This sort of problem was not the reason he had come West. He was a short, nervous man. His face still bore the wounds from his morning shave.

'I can't believe Sheriff Harrison is gone,' Stuart said.

All he could see was the sheriff lying in the middle of a

road on the deserted prairie, his horse standing nearby. He kept asking himself why. Harrison had gone to question Andrew Swearingen about the lynching. Maybe he was bringing Andrew in, and Andrew didn't want to be brought in. Maybe Andrew killed him. Suddenly Stuart no longer felt like a boy. He wanted to find Andrew. He would make him talk.

'Well, he is gone,' Payne said. 'There's no bringing him back. The question now is what are we going to do? Eloise, what we discuss doesn't need to be in the newspaper.'

'Our sheriff has been murdered,' she said. 'That's news. What goes on in here is news.'

'There's no arguing with that woman,' one of the councilmen said. 'You might as well accept that fact and move on.'

'Right now we're at the mercy of any murdering hoodlum that rides into town,' another said.

The man who spoke was Clarence Woodson, president of the Bank of Cheyenne. He wore a fine brown plaid suit, and he held an unlit cigar that he waved whenever he emphasized a point.

'I guarantee you every ne'er-do-well from here to California has heard that our sheriff is dead,' Woodson continued. 'They've all heard we're ripe for the picking. That's no offense to you, Zeke, but you're just one man. Harrison should have hired more deputies.'

I wonder what the president of the Bank of Cheyenne would say, Eloise thought, if he knew a man who rode with Jesse James was standing only a few feet from him. The thought led her to smile.

'What goes on here in this town is not really any of my business,' Owen said. 'Mr Mayor, I've already made myself clear on the matter. Nevertheless, since you insisted that I attend this gathering, I will say you asked a pertinent question a moment ago. What are you going to do? You've lost your sheriff. Your town needs a sheriff. You have a deputy. But you need a sheriff, and then your sheriff needs to hire deputies.'

Payne stared down at Stuart, whose eyes still appeared dazed. Him – a sheriff, he wanted to say. He's hardly more than a boy. Not too long ago he was walking behind a mule and a plow. Owen Chesterfield was right, though. The town needed a sheriff.

Stuart felt as if everyone was looking at him. He knew what they were thinking. He didn't have enough experience. He had never had to shoot at anyone. He had never even pulled his pistol on anyone. The men knew that. They wondered how he could confront coldblooded killers. And whoever killed Harrison was a coldblooded killer.

'Well, what about it, Zeke?' Payne asked. 'We need a sheriff. Are you up to the job?'

Not exactly a vote of confidence, Marcus thought. How can Stuart handle Swearingen and the other cattle barons? How can he handle a range war if it comes to that?

'You're damn right I'm up to the job,' Stuart said.

Stuart wanted to sound like a man, not like a boy in a man's clothing. He had to look like a man in charge. Inside, he was shaking.

'Take it easy, sonny,' Payne said.

'Don't call me sonny. Sheriff Harrison believed enough in me to hire me, didn't he? He thought I could do the job.'

'Well, the job's yours. But, as Mr Chesterfield has suggested, you're going to need some deputies.'

'What about you, Mr McPherson?' one of the councilmen asked. 'How about being a deputy?'

'Wonderful idea,' another said. 'It's no secret you know how to use a gun.'

'Mr McPherson, though abundantly qualified – you see,

he has had some experience with the law – is ready to head back East,' Owen said. 'He can't stay.'

'Mr McPherson, that's Mr Chesterfield talking,' Payne said. 'What do you say?'

Ezra walked out of the shadows and crossed the office – he did not stride quickly but there was determination in his gait – and stood in front of Stuart.

'Do you want me to help you?' Ezra said. 'I don't care what these other men say. You're the sheriff now. You're the one who has to decide.'

Stuart saw the Colt at Ezra's side. He remembered the train robbery. He remembered what Harrison had said. Ezra was the past that had returned to Cheyenne.

'I didn't like you the moment I saw you,' Stuart said. 'I don't know if I like you now. But I reckon I could use your help. I'd be obliged.'

'If Ezra is your deputy, then you need two deputies,' Owen said.

'I thought you're a Pinkerton,' Stuart said.

'I am. When I left Chicago, they told me to do what I need to do. This is what I need to do. Marcus, how about it? Do you need another job?'

'I think I'll stick to newspapering.'

'Zeke, take off that deputy's badge and give it to one of these gentlemen,' Payne said, and he reached into his coat pocket. 'Here's the sheriff's star. Slade gave it to me a little while ago. He said we might be needing it. Zeke, step up here.'

Stuart rose from the chair and walked past Ezra and stood at the desk. Payne pinned the badge onto Stuart's vest.

'Zeke, raise your right hand. Do you hereby swear to uphold the law here in Cheyenne, Wyoming?'

'I do.'

'Congratulations. You're now the sheriff. I'm sure there's another deputy's badge in a desk drawer.'

He walked to the back of the desk and pulled open a drawer.

'We're in luck,' he said, and he handed the badge to Owen. 'Well, what is this?'

He lifted a piece of paper and read.

'Damn,' he said. 'Mitch's letter of resignation. I had no idea he was planning to retire. For the life of me, I just can't understand how some things work out. Damn.'

Ezra and Owen walked along the sidewalk. Marcus, with Eloise beside him, followed. He was thankful to be out of the sheriff's office, away from the unbearable closeness, away from the heat trapped in the small room, away from the men who struggled to discover what to do. Stuart was not ready to be sheriff. Marcus was convinced of it. He was fortunate he would have someone like Ezra to guide him, to tell him what to do. He would just have to listen, and Marcus was not so sure the young sheriff of Cheyenne was willing to listen.

'Well, Ezra, how do you feel now that you're a deputy?' Owen asked.

'Same as I felt before I was a deputy.'

Two cowboys stumbled out of the Two Rivers and sang and shouted and staggered toward their horses. And then they were gone.

'I don't hear any piano music,' Owen said. 'Marcus, do you hear any piano music?'

'Can't say I do.'

'Were you wanting to dance?' Ezra said.

'Not with you, friend. I had Miss Endicott in mind.'

'I'm flattered, Mr Chesterfield.'

'I was pretty good in my day.'

A buggy raced down the street, past the dark window fronts, and stopped beside them. Luke gripped the reins tightly. Jennifer Beauchamp sat beside him.

'Where are you going in such a rush?' Ezra asked.

'Peter Swearingen came to get me. His wife is in labor. Jennifer and I are on our way.'

'Owen and I will catch up.'

In an instant the buggy was gone.

'I like how you speak for me,' Owen said. 'Are you sure you want to go back out there? Rayburn may be there this time.'

'Stokesbury, you coming?'

'Yeah, I'm coming.'

'Can you ride a horse?' Ezra asked.

'I'm going to ignore that question.'

'I'll tell Zeke where you're heading,' Eloise said.

The three men found Smitty in his small lean-to office.

'After Peter Swearingen came to me, wanting to know where he could find Doctor Tisdale, I had a feeling you gents might be needing horses. We'll get 'em saddled before you can say jack jabbit.'

They galloped out of town, past the gentlemen's club, past the quiet, small houses, past the city cemetery. Soon Marcus realized he had never seen anything so massive and so beautiful as the Wyoming prairie at night. The stars – and he thought there must have been at least a million of them – and a crescent moon lit the way. Beyond the prairie the mountains rose, dark and watchful. They crossed the Medicine Bow River, and the water splashed cold and refreshing against their legs. They caught up with the buggy. Jennifer held onto her bonnet with both hands.

They rode less than two hours, though it seemed to take much longer. The prairie was endless in the moonlight. Marcus wondered if all this land belonged to Swearingen, and he wondered why anyone would need so much land. Perhaps one day he would ask him – and then perhaps not.

Swearingen sat in a dark red wingchair in his study. He heard the shrieks from upstairs and he rose and walked to the sideboard and poured a glass of bourbon. He needed something, something to help him deal with the screams. Then he heard the horses. They were moving quickly up the long drive.

He rushed out of the study, down the hall, and onto the porch. Ginevra was already there. She held a small kerchief in her hands and she kept twisting it. She looked at her husband and smelled the alcohol. Luke jumped from the buggy and ran around to the other side and gave Jennifer his hand. Ezra and Ginevra looked at each other but did not speak.

'Luke, I can't tell you how grateful we all are,' Swearingen said.

'This is Jennifer Beauchamp. She's going to assist me.'

'I'm going to help too,' Ginevra said. 'We already have the water hot. I'll have it brought upstairs. Peter got back just a few minutes ago. He's upstairs with Anne.'

The three hurried inside. Ezra, Owen, and Marcus dismounted.

'Sir, I don't believe we've met,' Swearingen said.

'Owen Chesterfield's the name.'

'You men come inside for some refreshment,' Swearingen said. 'I'm sure you're thirsty after the long ride out here.'

'We don't turn down refreshment when it's free,' Owen said. 'It is free, isn't it, Mr Swearingen?'

'Free? Hell no. How do you think I made all my money? Not by giving stuff away. But come on in. I may change my mind.'

Swearingen laughed. He saw the outlines of two

cowboys standing next to the corral.

'Hey, you men, take care of these horses,' Swearingen called out.

He led Ezra, Owen and Marcus into the parlor.

'All the servants are busy with the baby, so I'll do the pouring myself. I trust whiskey is acceptable to everyone.'

'Water will be fine,' Ezra said.

'I'll take water also,' Marcus said.

'Whiskey will do just fine,' Owen said.

Peter came down the stairs and sat on the sofa near the front window. Swearingen held a glass toward him, but he shook his head. The others drank and listened. Shrieks spilled down the stairs, and Peter put his face in his hands.

'She's a tough one, Peter,' Swearingen said. 'She'll be all right.'

Sometimes even the tough ones don't make it, Marcus thought, and he suspected Peter might be thinking the same thing.

'Luke is a fine doctor,' Ezra said. 'Your wife is in good hands.'

'Pull off your coats, gentlemen,' Swearingen said. 'It's too hot to be formal.'

Swearingen lifted his glass but hesitated. In the dim light silver stars caught his attention. Both Ezra and Owen wore one.

'I didn't know you gentlemen had become enforcers of the law.'

'It wasn't something we planned,' Owen said. 'The situation just presented itself.'

'I know what you're talking about. Sometimes an opportunity, totally unexpected, comes along and you have to seize it. But I wasn't aware that Sheriff Harrison intended to hire anyone else.'

'Harrison is dead,' Ezra said.

Peter removed the hands from his face.

'Dead? But he was here this morning.'

'And I assure you,' Swearingen said, 'he was very much alive when he called on us.'

The clock on the mantel ticked, and Peter stood and walked to the hearth and then back to the sofa and then to the side window and back to the sofa and then to the hearth.

'Damn, boy, stop that pacing,' Swearingen said. 'You'd think you were nervous.'

On top of the mahogany table next to the chair where Owen sat lay a book. He reached into his coat pocket and withdrew a pair of wire-rimmed spectacles. He lifted the book and held it close to his eyes and then he moved it farther away, then farther.

'That's *Ben-Hur*,' Marcus said.

'Ben who?'

'*Ben-Hur*. It's a popular novel. A lot of people are reading it.'

'Have you read it?'

'Yes.'

'Did you like it?'

'Very much.'

'That's one of my wife's books,' Swearingen said. 'At night she always has a book in her hands.'

Owen flipped through the pages.

'I wish they made the words larger. A little hard for an old man like me to read.'

Ezra saw Owen's difficulty. Then Anne cried out, and Peter grabbed the edge of the mantel. Swearingen poured another glass of whiskey and handed it to his son.

'Here. Drink this. I insist. It'll help. It's going to be a long night.'

CHAPTER SEVEN

Rayburn stood in the darkness of an alley across the street from the jail. Earlier, as he sat at a table next to the window in the Three Rivers, he noticed Cheyenne's city councilmen bunched together on the sidewalk. They walked, it appeared to Rayburn, reluctantly toward the jail. He set his glass down on the table and followed. The alley was a good spot to observe what was happening.

He lit a cigarette and waited. He wondered what the discussion was about. Sooner or later he would find out, and then he would report to Swearingen. The door creaked open and the councilmen filed out. Well, they've got a bit more spring in their step, he said to himself. Something happened that seemed to please them.

Soon after the councilmen emerged, Ezra McPherson and Owen Chesterfield appeared, followed by Marcus Stokesbury and Eloise Endicott. They seemed to be in no particular hurry. Rayburn threw down the cigarette and crushed it beneath his boot.

Ezra McPherson. Rayburn recognized him, even in the darkness. Ezra McPherson was one man Rayburn thought he'd never lay eyes on again. But there he was. The only man Jesse James ever feared – or so the story went. You heard all kinds of stories. Still, Rayburn believed it. After

Ford killed Jesse, everyone, it seemed, expected McPherson to seek vengeance. Everyone in Missouri, it seemed, thought Rayburn had something to do with getting Ford to pull the trigger.

To those Rebs, I was just a no-good Yankee scoundrel, he thought. I could have told them I had nothing to do with Ford and Jesse, but it would have been absolutely pointless. I wish I had had something to do with it. Then I could have gotten a job in one of the traveling shows. I can hear the introduction: 'Ladies and gentlemen, here's the man who put an end to Jesse James.' I could have made good, easy money in one of the traveling shows.

Everyone expected McPherson to take care of Ford and then to come after Rayburn. In fact, Rayburn himself expected it. He sent men to eliminate that possibility, and the men did not return. The next day came, and then the next, and still there was no pursuit of vengeance.

'McPherson is just biding his time,' the people said.

Farmers came into town on Sundays for church, and Rayburn had ears among them. After the service was over, they huddled next to their wagons and buggies and speculated.

'Maybe Ezra is just waiting to see what Jesse's brother is going to do.'

'Yeah, well, you're forgetting Ezra quit riding with Jesse and Frank.'

'Yeah, that's true. I heard he was tired of the killing.'

'For him, the war was over.'

'How can it be over? How can it ever be over?'

'For Ezra, it was over.'

'Yeah, but that was before Ford killed Jesse. Now it ain't over.'

The days passed, and still Jesse's friend sought no vengeance. People said the waiting was making Ford crazy.

No one had seen McPherson for days. His neighbors got together and rode out to his farm. Maybe he was sick. Maybe one of his mules had kicked him and he couldn't get out of bed. But he was nowhere to be found. The house was empty. The barn was empty. No horses, no mules, no cows, no chickens.

'There's always chickens running around,' one said.

'There's nothing here. It's downright ghostly. What do you think happened?'

In the late afternoon sunlight Stitch Felker rode up on a sway-back mare and stared at the neighbors who huddled outside Ezra's house and spat tobacco juice and laughed.

'You men are a sorry, lazy sight for old eyes like mine,' Felker said. 'You ain't going to find Ezra McPherson anywhere around here.'

'What are you talking about, old coot? Do you know something we don't know?'

'I reckon I do. Ezra's gone. Gone for good. He's been gone for days. He has plum skedaddled. Before he left, he brought his span of mules over and gave them to me. You heard right, gents. He gave them to me. I've always said he had the finest span I've ever seen. He knew I'd take good care of them. "But, Ezra," I says, "where is you heading?" "I can't say," he says back. "But what about Ford?" I asks. "Ain't you going to kill him? There's not a jury in Missouri that'll convict you." He didn't answer. "Is Frank going to do it? Folks are actually placing bets on which one of you is going to pull the trigger." He still didn't answer. All he said was, "Whatever tack there is in the shop is yours. You've been a good friend, Stitch Felker," he says. And then he rode off. The blackness of the night clean swallowed him up. He warn't never much of a farmer. He was better with a Colt .45 than with a plow. All I can say is now I've got the finest span of mules in the county.'

Rayburn heard about the visit to the McPherson farm. He found it hard to believe, so he too rode out there. The door to the house stood open, as if it were inviting him to step inside. He kept his hand on his pistol, and he heeded the silent invitation. Nothing but darkness. A few chipped dishes cluttered the dry sink. A dirty linen towel lay nearby.

'Well, I reckon he is gone,' Rayburn said. 'I never thought he would just up and leave. But, by damn, that's what he's done.'

He walked outside and looked toward the barn. No point in going there, he thought. Ezra McPherson is gone. Those nosy neighbors were right. And they were right about something else. This place is ghostly.

The wind stirred and Rayburn felt uneasy. After Jesse James's death, Ezra McPherson was a threat. He had to be eliminated, so Rayburn sent a group of men to do the job. And every one of them is dead, he said to himself. Not a one came back alive. But maybe, just maybe, one of them got lucky before he breathed his last and put a bullet in old Ezra. Maybe old Ezra went off somewhere like a wounded dog to die. Maybe he is dead. That explains why this place feels haunted.

Rayburn shook his head. I don't need to think like that, he said to himself. If Ezra is dead, then there's nothing to worry about. His ghost sure as hell ain't going to bother me.

Now, standing across the street from the Cheyenne jail, Rayburn observed not a ghost, but Ezra McPherson himself. If I had a rifle, Rayburn thought, I could put a hole in him. But the time is not right. It will be, though. He shouldn't have come back. That was a mistake, and that mistake will get him killed.

Ezra and his companions walked down the sidewalk. Rayburn recognized the man walking alongside him. He did not remember the man's name. He had seen him a day or two before Ezra disappeared from Missouri. He must have had something to do with it. Rayburn heard the fellow had met with the governor. Again Rayburn thought about the ambush on a lonely country road. He had planned it carefully, yet somehow Ezra escaped. Rayburn suspected the man now walking alongside Ezra must have had something to do with that too.

A buggy hurried down the street. It was Luke Tisdale and the schoolteacher. He had heard about her. She had come from South Carolina with her boy. She was the sister of Silas Taylor's wife. It was interesting that she would be going for a buggy ride with the young Tisdale at this time of night.

'Well, I reckon since her old man is dead, she's looking for a little companionship with the young Tisdale.'

They talked. Rayburn couldn't hear, but there seemed to be some urgency. Then the buggy was gone, and so were the others.

Rayburn reached for another cigarette and a match. He stopped before striking it on the leather sole of his boot. Two riders approached, slowly, almost as if they were not moving. At the end of the street they looked small and, at first, he did not recognize them.

'I don't believe what I'm seeing.'

Andrew Swearingen and Curly Pike rode past the Two Rivers. Andrew looked at the light escaping from one of the upstairs windows. Rose would be in the room, and she probably would not be alone. He thought about Sven. He remembered the young farmer reaching for the old pistol tucked in his belt. He remembered feeling the Colt in his own hand and feeling the trigger. Then the farmer lay on the floor.

'What you're doing is crazy,' Curly said. 'I swear being in

71

the sun so long has done something to your brain.'

They stopped in front of the jail and dismounted and tied the reins to the hitching post. The town was quiet, quieter than they had ever heard it. They heard no laughter, no piano music. Curly didn't like it. It reminded him of the quiet before a twister. Andrew unbuckled his gun belt.

'Andrew, don't do this,' Curly said.

'I've been a part of the bloodshed. Maybe I can keep more of it from happening.'

'And maybe there are frozen snowballs in hell.'

After the meeting with the city councilmen, Stuart persuaded himself to sit behind the desk. He figured it was something Harrison would have wanted him to do. He was the sheriff now. He should sit where the sheriff was supposed to sit. He did not sit long. Eloise Endicott came into the office. Years ago his mother had told him, 'Boy, when a lady enters the room, you stand up. Show that you've got some manners.' He stood and couldn't help smiling. His mother would be proud.

'Your new deputies are accompanying Doctor Tisdale out to the Swearingen ranch,' Eloise said. 'Anne Tisdale is in labor.'

'Is she in danger?'

'I don't know.'

'Sheriff Harrison went out there this morning. He didn't come back.'

'Don't worry about Ezra.'

'You think he's something special, don't you?'

'Yes, I do.'

'Well, Miss Endicott, I'm beginning to think that myself. I sure hope things stay quiet while they're gone.'

'I'm sure there's nothing to worry about. I doubt anything unexpected will happen tonight.'

The door swung open and Andrew and Curly walked in.

'I'm not here to cause any trouble,' Andrew said.

'You've already caused enough trouble,' Stuart said. 'Why did you do it?'

'I should have stopped it. I should have at least tried. I knew that boy wasn't a cattle rustler. He didn't deserve to hang. Go get Sheriff Harrison.'

'Sheriff Harrison is dead.'

'Dead?'

'You heard me.'

'I don't understand.'

'No, of course you don't.'

'You don't think I had anything to do with it?'

'He rode out to your place early this morning. He wanted to talk to you about the lynching. He never came back. Somebody shot and killed him.'

'I've got blood on my hands. I don't deny that. But it's not Harrison's.'

'Why have you come traipsing in here?'

'I didn't do anything to stop the lynching. I should have. I'm not going to run.'

'Are you going to tell me who else was involved?'

'No.'

'So you want to take all the blame? Is that the way it is?'

'Yes, I reckon so.'

'And you – you look guiltier than him. Did you have anything to do with it?'

Curly shook his head.

'Andrew, leave your gun belt on the desk.'

It takes a lot to surprise me, Eloise thought, but I'm surprised. Both Andrew and Curly avoided her eyes.

Stuart led Andrew through the back door to one of the three cells. He closed the cell door and turned the key in the lock. Andrew sat on the narrow bed and stared at the floor.

'It's like a tomb back here,' Andrew said.

'You complaining about our accommodations?'

'No, I'm not complaining. I feel like this is where I should be.'

'You need anything? Any water?'

'No. I'm fine.'

The cell was hot. No air stirred. Pale moonlight fell through the one barred window. Stuart turned to leave, but he hesitated.

'Killing that farmer in the Two Rivers did something to you, didn't it?'

'Have you ever killed anyone, Zeke?'

'No. You were eager to. I'm not.'

Curly walked both horses down the street toward the livery. The storefronts were black. The lights in the saloons were dim. From the shadows a man stepped into the middle of the street.

'What are you doing in town, Rayburn?'

'Oh, I come into town occasionally to see what's going on, and I just saw something going on. I just don't know exactly what. I expect you to tell me. What went on in there?'

'In where?'

'Don't play games with me, Curly. You went in the sheriff's office with Andrew. Only you came out.'

'Andrew turned himself in.'

'He did what?'

'He's taking the blame for the lynching.'

'He's lost his mind. Did he say who else—'

'He's not interested in naming any names.'

'Well, I'll be damned. I can imagine what his old man is going to say about this.'

'Zeke Stuart told us Sheriff Harrison is dead. Zeke is the sheriff now. You don't look too surprised to hear about

Harrison.'

'I'm sure Harrison had his enemies. He was a lawman a long time. Are you heading back to the ranch?'

'No.'

'What do you mean, no?'

'Just that. I quit.'

'I didn't take you for a man who quits. What's the problem? Ain't we paying you enough money?'

'You're paying enough.'

'Then what's eating you?'

'I figure it's time to move on.'

'Don't you want the money that's owed you?'

'Keep the money.'

'Deserting Swearingen isn't the smartest thing to do. You ought to know that.'

'I ain't afraid of Swearingen, and I ain't afraid of you.'

'You're a fool, Curly Pike. I thought you had more sense. But you're a fool, a damn fool.'

'Say what you want, Rayburn. I'm through with you.'

CHAPTER EIGHT

Curly led the horses past Rayburn, past Rayburn's sudden laughter that vanished just as suddenly, but not past the silence. It clung to the storefronts, to the sidewalks. Down the street stood the gentlemen's club. He looked up at the second floor windows, as black as the night itself. He knew that eyes were watching – and waiting.

I need a drink, he thought. He glanced over his shoulder. Rayburn was gone. The Two Rivers beckoned. He tied the horses to the hitching post.

'You two ladies just wait here a bit,' he said, and he entered the saloon.

'I didn't expect to see you this late,' Dooley said from behind the bar.

'Well, it's your lucky night. Where's the piano player?'

'Things are so quiet he decided to go home. I'm not sure I've ever seen it this quiet. Whatcha having?'

'Whiskey.'

'Want the bottle?'

'No, just a glass.'

Curly avoided the floor where the farmer had lain – some of Andrew's handiwork, he said to himself – and sat at a table in the far corner and gripped the glass tightly in his hands. Keeping the bottle was tempting, but he needed to think. Even without the whiskey little was clear. He realized he had never been the only customer in the Two Rivers before.

An occasional laugh or giggle came from one of the upstairs rooms. Maybe that's what I need, he thought, but he quickly dismissed the idea.

'I don't have a job,' he said. 'I got to watch my money.'

Rose walked down the stairs, the straps of a long faded red dress hanging loosely on her shoulders. She saw Curly and went to the table.

'Cowboy, buy me a drink?'

He did not look up and she walked to the bar and Dooley poured a glass.

'What's wrong with him?' she asked.

'I don't know. He hasn't said much since he's been in here. Watch yourself. I don't trust him.'

She took the glass and came back to Curly's table. Her left cheek bore a purplish bruise.

'You want some company?'

'If you're talking about the kind of company you provide upstairs, the answer is no. I got to be careful with the few dollars I got left.'

She pulled back a chair and sat.

'I thought Swearingen pays you men well. Forty a month. That's what I've heard. That's more than what most cowpokes like you make.'

'I don't give a damn about his money. I quit today.'

'My, my. You're a brave man, Curly Pike. Walking away from Swearingen can get a man killed. Just ask John Tisdale.'

'I don't want to talk about John Tisdale.'

Dooley brought a bottle to the table.

'You sure you don't want this?'

'I'm sure.'

'Set it down, Dooley,' she said. 'He needs it. He took a big step today. He quit his job.'

'You quit Swearingen? If Swearingen doesn't kill you, Rayburn will. I thought you were smarter than that.'

'Dooley, I ain't interested in what you think. Take the damn bottle. I don't want it.'

'Maybe I do,' Rose said.

Dooley returned to the bar and picked up a towel to dry a glass. He kept his eyes on Curly. Men like him were unpredictable.

'Where's your friend Andrew?' she asked.

'He's around.'

'In town?'

'Yes, in town.'

'I guess he's found someone else to comfort him.'

'Maybe.'

'To hell with him.'

'You ought to pay him a visit.'

'Why would I do a thing like that?'

'I'm sure he'd love to see you.'

'And if I get a hankering to see him, where can I find him?'

'Just up the street. The jail.'

Rose set the glass down.

'Rose, is there trouble?' Dooley asked, and he reached for the shotgun behind the bar.

'There's no trouble,' she said. 'Why is he in jail?'

'He thinks that's where he belongs.'

'Yeah, well, I agree. You saw what he did to Sven Burleson.'

'The Swede didn't give him much choice.'

'Andrew could've walked away. He didn't have to kill that dumb homesteader.'

'There's no point in going over it again, Rose. Sven is

dead. Andrew is in jail, and it has nothing to do with Sven being dead.'

'I don't understand. Why don't you come upstairs and explain it to me?'

'Like I said, I don't have money for that. What's the matter with you? You deaf?'

'I've got something that's better than whiskey. It'll make you feel like you're in a wonderful world. The world we live in, Curly Pike, is not wonderful. What I have upstairs will make you forget all your troubles, all your pain. Later, you'll thank me.'

'I'm not interested in your dope.'

'Who said anything about dope?'

'I know what you're doing. Everybody knows. That stuff will kill you.'

'What if it does? What's it to you?'

'It ain't nothing to me,' Curly said. 'Fat whores are nothing to me.'

'You know what you are, Curly Pike? You're just a worthless cowboy. You don't have a home. You've probably never had a home. You don't have anyone who cares whether you live or die. If you've got a momma, I bet she never thinks about you. She never wonders where you are. You've never amounted to anything, and you never will. You think calling me a whore makes you better than me? I've got news, buddy boy. It don't.'

'You oughtta get into politics, Rose. You've got a natural gift for speech-making. If I'm still in Cheyenne, I'll vote for you. Run for mayor. You'll make history.'

He lifted the glass as a toast.

'Here's to the first fat whore to be elected mayor of Cheyenne.'

'Go to hell, you mangy bastard.'

Rose stood and grabbed hold of the table to steady

herself. A fog descended on the saloon and she was not sure where the stairs were. Somehow her small feet found them, and she climbed. At one moment the stairs veered to the right, the next moment to the left. She looked down at the bar. Nothing but yellow light.

'Rose, you all right?' Dooley called.

She clutched the banister and climbed and thought the stairs would never end. Once inside her room, she went to the pine dresser and pulled the top drawer. It was stuck. She pulled harder, and there it was. A Remington rimfire derringer. A gift from Madame Marie in St. Louis long ago. Barrel over barrel. Rose always kept it loaded.

'Hold onto this,' Madame Marie said. 'One of these days, if you stay in this business long enough, you'll need it.'

Rose did not remember much about Madame Marie. Curly would have thought she was fat too. That much she did remember about Madame Marie. And then she remembered more. She looked sick. Maybe she was.

Rose held the derringer in the pale light and stared at the shiny barrels.

'Madame Marie said I'll need you. How right she was.'

The gunshot shattered the quiet, and Curly nearly jumped out of his chair. Dooley hurried around the corner of the bar and ran up the stairs. The door to Rose's room was ajar, and he went in.

'Oh, no! Oh, God, no! Rose, no!'

Curly's hand trembled. He did not finish his drink.

CHAPTER NINE

Curly Pike stood at the back door of the gentlemen's club and looked about him, as if someone might be watching. All the other buildings were silent, black. The door opened and Schultz stood in the darkness of the hall. To Curly, Schultz looked old, too old to leave the comforts of the East and to establish a large cattle spread. It was not anything like Swearingen's spread, but it was big enough. Schultz looked past Curly.

'Don't be so concerned,' Curly said. 'I ain't been followed.'

'Are you sure?'

'Hell, yes, I'm sure.'

'The others are upstairs. We've been waiting.'

'I wanted to make sure all your hired help went home.'

'No one else is here. You won't be seen.'

'That's the way I like it.'

They walked down the carpeted hall and up the stairs. At the top of the stairs Schultz went to a door and knocked one time. Then he pushed it open and stepped aside so that Curly could enter. A lamp sitting on a table in the far corner did little to dispel the darkness. Palmer sat in a chair near the cold fireplace, and Lansing stood at the window. He turned and nodded briefly and then looked back at the street below. Meeting with Swearingen's fellow cattle barons made Curly uneasy. He had told Schultz he had not been followed, but was he sure? He had to make it seem he was sure, but Rayburn was in town. You didn't always see him coming until it was too late.

'So young Andrew Swearingen has turned himself in,' Lansing said.

'How do you know?' Curly asked.

'Schultz, get Mr Pike something to drink. I'm sure he's thirsty.'

'I've been drinking already.'

'Then drink some more.'

Curly sat in a plush chair in the middle of the room and took the whiskey and drank. A little smoother than what he got at the Two Rivers.

'Can we get some more light in here?'

'I can see just fine. After a while, you grow accustomed to the darkness. I heard a pistol shot. It sounded like a der-ringer.'

'It came from the Two Rivers. Apparently one of the whores got tired of living. Maybe she wasn't getting enough business.'

'That's too bad.'

Lansing left the window and took a chair across from him. Only a few feet separated them. Lansing was much younger than the other two, yet he called the shots. He gave the orders, and the others obeyed.

'Would you like a cigar?' Lansing asked.

'No.'

Curly set the glass on the floor.

'I'm sure the new sheriff was surprised to have a pris-oner so soon, especially one named Swearingen.'

'He was surprised, all right.'

'Swearingen will come for his son,' Lansing said. 'He will ride into town, probably with a few of his men, a few of his hired guns, and Rayburn most certainly will accompany him. Swearingen will attempt to free his son. Cheyenne hasn't seen such excitement in a long time.'

'I don't like the sound of this,' Palmer said. 'There's going to be a war out there. We're going to get caught in the middle. We should get out of town now.'

'Not so fast,' Lansing said. 'This is exactly what we want.'

'I don't follow,' Schultz said.

'We have an opportunity to let the whole world know who killed John Tisdale. That has been a mystery for much too long. It's time we shed light on the mystery, and then we simply let the aggrieved parties proceed to sort things out. Meanwhile, we just sit back and watch.'

'Wait a minute,' Curly said. 'You said Tisdale's killer would remain invisible—'

'Don't worry, Curly,' Lansing said. 'Your secret – our secret – is safe. When Swearingen and his men ride into town, I just want you to let it be known to everyone that Rayburn did the infamous deed. I want you to make a big announcement so that everyone hears. That will set everything into motion. And then – it's important that you remember this, Curly – get out of the way. Bullets, I assure you, will be flying. I wouldn't want you to get hurt. If things go as I expect, Swearingen will catch one of the bullets. People will say that Rayburn was acting on Swearingen's orders. I don't want him to have an opportunity to defend himself in court. He's too smart. He'll have a smart attorney. If Ezra McPherson is as good with a pistol as I hear he is, he'll take care of Swearingen. I love making plans and seeing them work out.'

Lansing laughed.

'I don't see any humor,' Schultz said.

'Nor do I,' Palmer said.

'Of course not. Both of you are much too serious. You're

too serious about life. You're too serious about yourselves.'

Lansing laughed so hard that tears wet his face. He pulled a handkerchief to wipe them, and still he laughed. Schultz and Palmer glanced at each other.

'So you want me to stand between the sheriff and Swearingen's men and say that Rayburn is the one who killed Tisdale,' Curly said.

'Don't stop there,' Lansing said. 'You might as well add that he murdered Sheriff Harrison, too. It's certainly believable. No one will doubt you, Curly. You will be perceived as a hero, a man determined to see that justice is done.'

'You're crazy,' Curly said. 'I didn't realize it until now, but you're absolutely crazy. There are institutions for men like you. You should be in one.'

'It's a crazy world we live in, Curly. I've learned to adapt. And, unless I'm mistaken, I believe you're on the road to learning how to adapt. Men like us will survive. Men like Swearingen and Rayburn – well, they are bound for extinction.'

'You're wrong, Lansing,' Curly said. 'If I'm caught in the middle of a gunfight, I'm bound for extinction. Why the hell don't I just walk into the jail and tell the sheriff that Rayburn killed Tisdale and Harrison?'

'If you were to do that, Curly, no one would see you. Where would the drama be? I want the whole damn world – at least Cheyenne – to hear your pronouncement. Trust me, Curly. After this is all over, you'll find yourself a leading citizen of Wyoming. Men will shake your hand. Men will slap you on the back. Men will point you out to their sons. Years from now a monument will be erected in your honor. Of course, by then you'll be dead.'

'I still think you're crazy.'

Lansing motioned to Schultz, who went to a mahogany

sideboard and brought back a small cowhide bag pulled tight at the top with rawhide and handed it to Curly. The sack was heavy.

'Gold coins,' Lansing said. 'I know how much you like gold. What's in that sack says I'm not as crazy as you think and you're going to do what I'm telling you to do.'

Curly stood and held the bag firmly, as if at any moment Lansing would decide to take it back. He started for the door but stopped.

'Lansing, how did you know the sheriff would ride out to see Swearingen?'

'I just figured he would. And you did what you were instructed to do.'

'This web that you're weaving – you must really have it in for Swearingen.'

'Curly, my motivations are not any of your affair.'

'What'd he do, anyway – become too friendly with your wife?'

Curly smiled a smile that quickly vanished. Lansing suddenly was only inches from his face. The skin was pulled tight across his face, so tight Curly thought he was confronting a skeleton.

'Get out, Curly. You don't want to make me angry, do you?'

Curly went to the back door and opened it slowly. He expected Rayburn to be waiting for him. He might ask a question or two and then there would be a gunshot. He pulled his pistol and stepped into the alley.

'If you're out here, Rayburn, show yourself.'

No answer came. Curly sought the darkness of another alley, a safe place where he would count his money.

Schultz and Palmer lifted their derbies from the hall tree.

'What's the hurry, gentlemen?' Lansing asked. 'Don't

leave town. Stay and see the show.'

'I'd rather not,' Palmer said.

Palmer and Schultz went out of the front door and looked up and down the street. In the distance the shadow of Curly Pike stumbled into the darkness.

'Pike doesn't know how right he is,' Palmer said.

'What do you mean?'

'Back in New York Lansing put together a deal to move into the garment district. He had a lot of money at stake. He heard Swearingen was doing the same thing. Lansing met with John Tisdale, tried to get him to reveal all of Swearingen's strategy, but Tisdale wouldn't do it. Lansing offered him a lot of money, even offered him a job. Still, Tisdale wouldn't budge. Lansing doesn't like being told no. While he was trying to get information from Tisdale, Swearingen was getting information from Lansing's wife.'

'Are you serious?'

'Oh, yes, I'm serious. Swearingen has told me about it. He was quite pleased with himself. He cornered the market, and Lansing was left out in the cold. Have you ever seen Lansing's boy?'

'No.'

'Well, he doesn't much look like Lansing. He doesn't have Lansing's gaunt face. He looks like somebody else.'

'Do you think Tisdale knew what Swearingen was doing?'

'I don't know. Probably not. But Lansing believed he did.'

'Why didn't he divorce her? New York society would have understood.'

'He would have felt humiliated,' Palmer said. 'Besides, her family's money is older than his. He needs her to open certain doors he cannot open. But at least he can get through them. Swearingen will never be able to.'

'Lansing has come a long way to get revenge. I wonder why he needs us.'

'He doesn't, not really. It's all smoke. He wants to give the impression of a united front to deal with the home-steaders, a united front that includes Swearingen. No one will suspect what he is really doing.'

'Swearingen is smart. He'll figure it out.'

'By then, it will be too late.'

'Pike is right about something else,' Schultz said.

'Yeah?'

'Lansing is crazy. After he deals with Swearingen, if he decides he wants our land, what sort of web will he spin for us?'

'I don't know about you, but I'm going back to New York.'

'Do you think you'll be safe in New York?'

'I'll take my chances there.'

CHAPTER TEN

Sunlight was two hours away from sliding across the window sills, and Swearingen shifted his large body in the chair. He was stiff. Rising to his feet seemed impossible, but a horse was coming up the drive. Ezra, Marcus, and Owen appeared to be asleep. He did not understand how anyone could sleep with the moans and screams from upstairs. Peter sat with his face in his hands.

Swearingen fixed his large hands on the arms of the chair and struggled to his feet. Peter looked up. His eyes were red.

'I've got to get some fresh air,' the big man said. 'Do you want to come?'

'No. I'll stay here.'

Swearingen walked into the hall and out of the front door. One of the ranch hands kept a dog, and the dog started barking. Someone shouted for it to shut up and it did. The rider headed to the barn.

'Rayburn is keeping long hours,' Swearingen said.

The foreman came out of the barn and walked toward the house. In the blackness of the night he was barely visible.

'Out for a little ride?' Swearingen asked.

'I rode into town. I like to find out if there's any news worth knowing.'

'Is there?'

'Yeah, you might say there is.'

'Are you going to keep me guessing?'

'The worthy members of the town council had a little meeting in the sheriff's office. It had to be an awfully important meeting because the newspaper lady was there. I can't tell you what they said. For some reason they didn't invite me. I found out – later – that Sheriff Harrison is dead. Have you heard? I can tell you one thing – the sheriff's untimely demise apparently hit the councilmen pretty hard.'

'I would expect that. Yeah, I heard about Harrison awhile ago. Rayburn, I wanted you to talk to Harrison. I didn't want you to kill him.'

'Why is it every time somebody gets killed I get blamed?'

'I can't imagine.'

'Anyway, Zeke Stuart is wearing the sheriff's badge. That should make everyone sleep well.'

'He's not the only one wearing a badge. He has help.'

'What are you talking about?'

'Two deputies are inside the house right now,' Swearingen said. 'That fellow McPherson and his companion, Chesterfield.'

'You're telling me they're deputies?'

'You look concerned, Rayburn. I'm not paying you to get scared.'

'I'm well aware of what you're paying me for, and, I have to say, you're getting your damn money's worth. You got any complaints?'

'I have no complaints.'

Swearingen turned, but Rayburn ran up the steps and grabbed his arm.

'You haven't heard all my news,' Rayburn said. 'I saw Andrew.'

'Where? What's he doing? Was he with Rose again?'

'He rode into town. But not to see Rose. Just as pretty as you please, he rode right up to the sheriff's office. Curly

Pike was with him. It seems your son has turned himself in. At least he's making himself comfortable in a cell.'

Swearingen felt weak. He could not believe what Rayburn had just said. Surely Ginevra had not advised their son to go to jail, he thought. She had confused him. He wasn't thinking straight.

'He turned himself in? For what? Why would he do such a thing?'

'I talked with Curly. He says your son's taking the blame for the lynching of that farm boy. I don't think he liked seeing that farm boy who rustled some of your cattle swinging at the end of a rope. Andrew doesn't have the stomach for that sort of thing. I want you to understand something, Swearingen.'

'Just what is it you want me to understand?'

'Andrew had better not do any talking. To make this country profitable for men like you, certain steps, as we know, have to be taken. They're not always pleasant. And they're not always within the strictest confines of the law. But they're steps that have to be taken. That means no one needs to do any talking to the law. Can I make myself any clearer?'

'Rayburn, I don't like your tone. You do what I'm paying you to do, and you won't have anything to worry about. My son is not doing any talking, as you put it. Something crazy has gotten into his head, and he needs our help. We have to get him out. No son of mine is going to stay in jail. After this damn baby gets born, we're riding into town to get him out. Pick some men we can trust. Just a few. I don't want to stir up any more trouble than is necessary. But I want these men to be able to handle a gun.'

'I've never broken a man out of jail who wants to be in jail.'

Swearingen went into the house and slammed the door. Suddenly, silently, a figure emerged from the shadows at the end of the porch. From the corner of his eye Rayburn saw and jumped back and stumbled down the steps and fell. He stood and the man hovered above him.

'You're nervous,' Ezra said. 'Don't worry. I'm not going to kill you here. It's not the time. It's not the place. But I will kill you.'

'To hell you will. A dog that turns tail and runs ain't going to kill nobody.'

'You killed John Tisdale. You killed Sheriff Harrison.'

'You don't know what you're talking about. I didn't kill either one of them.'

'You were responsible for Jesse's murder.'

'Ford took care of that. I didn't have anything to do with it. McPherson, go back to where you ran to. This ain't no place for you.'

'You tried to have me killed. You hired men to do it. You didn't have the guts to do it yourself.'

'You're crazy. I didn't try to have you killed. If I had tried, believe me – you wouldn't be standing here now.'

Owen came onto the porch and stretched his arms and yawned.

'Ezra, they've made some breakfast for us. Come on inside. Besides, there's a bad smell out here.'

'Watch your tongue, old man,' Rayburn said.

'We're officers of the law,' Owen said, and he pulled his coat back to show the badge. 'You're the one who'd better watch what you say. You threaten us, bud, and you'll be on your way to the calaboose.'

Rayburn backed away into the darkness. The red tip of a cigarette flew into the air and landed in the dirt.

'Ezra, the biscuits are getting cold.'

'He killed John Tisdale. He killed Harrison. I'm convinced of it.'

'You know it, and I know it, and probably the whole town

knows it. But knowing it and proving it aren't quite the same.'

'I don't have to prove it. When the time comes, I'm going to kill him. I made a mistake, Owen. I let him live. Before I left Missouri, I should have killed him. But it's not too late. At least I've given him something to think about.'

'Wait till after breakfast before you do any more killing. They've got eggs and ham in there. I know all about your reputation. You don't like to do any killing on an empty stomach.'

'Owen, I wanted to leave all the killing behind me. You do believe that, don't you? I'm trying to make myself believe it, but it's hard. And now I find Rayburn, a snake if there ever was one.'

'Folks in Missouri used to tell me you were born with a six-shooter in your hand.'

'I guess they were right. When I went to Jekyll Island, when I lived beside the ocean, I found a peace I had never known before. The salt in the ocean breeze seemed to cleanse me of the violence. There was joy waking up in the morning, something I hadn't experienced in a long time. I wish I could have stayed there, but I couldn't let Luke come out here by himself. He's hotheaded sometimes. I was afraid he might end up like his brother. And as soon as I came back here, I had to kill those train robbers. And now there's going to be more killing. I can't escape it.'

Owen lay a hand on his shoulder.

'Maybe it won't be as bad as you think. You know, we can ride into town and put these badges down on the sheriff's desk and catch the Union Pacific for points East.'

'I can't do that.'

'I can slap handcuffs on the young Doctor Tisdale and charge him with being a threat to the peace and escort him back to Jekyll Island.'

'I don't think you can charge him with anything.

Besides, I think he's in love with that young woman who's helping him right now.'

'It must be wonderful to be young and to be in love.'

'It is.'

'Well, you may still be in love with that woman upstairs who just happens to be married to the wealthiest rancher in Wyoming, but you're not young. Put the past behind you and move on.'

'When I move on, the past is right behind me.'

'Well, keep it behind you.'

'Swearingen and Rayburn were talking about Andrew Swearingen, but I couldn't make out what they were saying.'

'Where is that boy?'

'Hopefully a long way from here. Owen, why didn't you tell me about your eyes?'

'What's to tell?'

'You can't see too well.'

'I can see well enough.'

'How long have they been bothering you?'

'We're both getting old, Ezra. Things like this happen. Come on. Food's getting cold.'

Owen turned and went into the hall. Ezra remained on the porch. His hand rested on the Colt at his side.

Eloise Endicott sat at her desk in the newspaper office and scribbled notes on a piece of paper. She had her lead story for the next edition. Cattle baron's son turns himself in. It should make for interesting reading, she thought. Swearingen would not be happy.

She thought about the other cattle barons. They might not be as wealthy as Swearingen. Their spreads might not be as large as his. Still, they were a force to be reckoned with. If they sensed any kind of weakness in Swearingen, they, like a pack of wolves, would attack. She knew it, and so did Swearingen. He had sought to establish a kingdom in Wyoming, and she sensed that it was slowly disintegrating. On the one hand, Swearingen would have to defend himself against the other ranchers. On the other hand, he would have to deal with the homesteaders who refused to be intimidated.

'One thing's for sure,' she said. 'There'll be plenty to write about.'

She needed to interview Andrew. Perhaps Zeke Stuart would not permit an interview. Because he was new on the job, he would be concerned about protocol, but she would try. She needed to find out why Andrew wanted to seek a jail cell instead of the safety of his father's money.

Footsteps came down the sidewalk. She opened a desk drawer and gripped the pistol that lay there. The door opened and Lawrence Byrd walked in. She shut the drawer.

'Why isn't my only reporter getting some rest?' she asked.

'Couldn't sleep.'

He removed his derby and sat in the chair in front of her desk.

'The town is quiet tonight,' he said. 'It's been quiet many times before, I guess, but tonight it's different. There's something about it that's disquieting.'

'You do like a play on words.'

'Well, it is unsettling.'

She was fond of Byrd. He had a youthful energy, a determination that shone in the pursuit of a story. A younger version of Marcus Stokesbury, she thought. Tonight, though, he did not seem himself. The energy was not there.

'What's troubling you?' she asked.

'When you walk past the gentlemen's club, especially at

night, do you ever get the feeling someone is watching you? Do you ever get the feeling someone is paying attention to everything that occurs on the streets of Cheyenne?'

'You have a vivid imagination.'

'I guess. Earlier tonight I saw Curly Pike, that ranch hand from Swearingen's. He was heading into the Two Rivers. I don't think he saw me. I thought it was a bit strange that he would be in town so late. Then I ran into his foreman, Rayburn. I mean I literally ran into him on the sidewalk. He was in a hurry. We nearly knocked each other down. I apologized for not watching where I was going. He said nothing. Eloise, you should have seen his face. It was all drawn up in anger. I thought for a moment he was going to pull his pistol on me. And then he brushed past me. But the look on his face – well, when I went to the boarding house and lay down, I couldn't sleep. I kept seeing his face. Something's going to happen. I don't know exactly what, but it's not going to be good.'

Soon Swearingen will know that his younger son is in jail, she thought. She would like to observe him when he received the news. He's like a volcano, she thought, and is about to explode.

'Andrew Swearingen is in jail,' she said.

'In jail? What did he do?'

'Apparently he had something to do with a lynching.'

'The Darton boy.'

'Yes, I suppose so. The strange thing is he wants to take all the blame.'

'That is strange. I guess a guilty conscience got the best of him. Judge Henry is not in town. He won't be back for at least two weeks.'

'A lot can happen in two weeks,' she said.

'A lot can happen before sunrise.'

CHAPTER ELEVEN

Marcus walked slowly about the room. He carried a cup of coffee from the breakfast one of Swearingen's servants had prepared. The moans and screams from upstairs came more quickly. Peter once again paced from his chair to the hearth, so Marcus sat down. Two men pacing would be a little too much, he decided. He figured the labor would not last much longer. By no means did he consider himself an expert on such matters, but it was just a feeling he had.

Swearingen paid no attention to Peter. In fact, he seemed oblivious to him. Instead, he stared at Ezra. Marcus was curious. He wondered why the rancher would focus so intently on his visitor. On Swearingen's face a red fury mustered its strength. Ezra had his hat pulled low over his eyes, so he did not see. Perhaps he knew. Somehow, Marcus thought, a man like Ezra would know when he was being watched.

For some reason – and he did not understand why – Marcus thought about Atlanta, about the newspaper not far from Union Station. He thought about the vibration of the wood floors as the presses ran, mighty, implacable. And then he knew. He was ready to return. He had always wanted to see the West, and now he had seen it. It was time to go back. Besides, his editor might decide that the newspaper could operate just fine without him.

He thought that, immediately after the baby was born, immediately after riding back to Cheyenne, he would buy his ticket. Yet he knew he would not. As hard as it is to admit, he said to himself, I have to remain in Cheyenne. There's more to the story I've been chasing. If I tell Wilcox there's more to the story, I know what he will say.

'Marcus, don't come back until you have all of it.'

The cry of a baby reached the parlor and Peter jumped from his chair and ran into the hall. Luke, his white shirt sleeves rolled up, slowly descended the stairs.

'You have a strong, healthy baby boy.'

'And Anne? Is Anne all right?'

'She's exhausted, and that's not surprising. The baby wore her out. The baby wore all of us out. She's going to need some rest, but she'll be fine. Why don't you go upstairs? Your family wants to see you.'

Peter hurried up the stairs. Ezra stood at the parlor door.

'You did real good, Doctor Tisdale.'

'Jennifer was such a help. She and Mrs Swearingen were such a comfort to Anne.'

'Did I hear my name mentioned?'

Jennifer came down the stairs. Her blonde hair hung loosely above her shoulders. Her face was red from the heat of the upstairs bedroom. Luke took her hand and led her down the hall and out of the door.

'Well, I'll be damned,' Swearingen said from his chair by the hearth. 'I'm a grandfather. The financial market in New York should respond favorably to this news. What do you think, Chesterfield?'

'I think you should not forget about London,' Owen said.

'Wire a story to your editor in Atlanta, Stokesbury,'

Swearingen said. 'Tell him I'm so happy I think I'll buy the whole damn state of Georgia.'

'There's still a bit of Wyoming left,' Owen said.

'Hell, I'll buy it too.'

Luke and Jennifer stood in the grassless yard in front of the porch steps.

'We need to head back to town,' he said. 'Peter's mother can handle things now. If they need us, they can send a rider. But I think Anne will be all right.'

'You were marvelous,' Jennifer said.

'There's no need to say that.'

'But you were. It was a difficult delivery. You and I both know it. At one point I wasn't sure – well, I wasn't sure if Anne was going to have the strength to make it.'

'You held her hand and talked to her and that gave her strength. It was something I couldn't give.'

'You have a special gift. You should have seen your face – the moment you held the baby in the lamplight so that Anne could see him. Your face had a look of utter satisfaction, happiness.'

He took her into his arms and held her tightly and kissed her.

'Is that my reward for being a great help?' she asked.

'Jennifer, I'm not a poet. I can't say the things you need to hear. But what I can say is that I'm in love with you. I think I've been in love with you since I first saw you on the train.'

'Well, Doctor Tisdale, you have to remember that we have a professional relationship. I have assisted you in your medical duties. Emotion should not enter into it.'

Again he kissed her.

'And then,' she said, 'perhaps it should. Yes, Doctor Tisdale, now that I've thought about it, emotion should definitely enter into it.'

Swearingen lifted a crystal decanter from the buffet and poured whiskey. He and Ezra and Owen and Marcus raised their glasses.

'Here's to the next generation,' he said.

'May it be a heap sight better than this one,' Owen said.

'It won't have to try too hard,' Ezra said.

Ginevra walked into the parlor and sat without speaking. Ezra stared at her. She looked tired, more tired than Jennifer, and he wanted to go to her. He wanted to tell her that she had fulfilled her responsibilities in this house and that she should leave with him. He wanted to tell Swearingen that he would never see her again.

'Some girls from the kitchen are upstairs looking after things,' she said.

'Dear, you look so tired one would think you're the one who had the baby,' Swearingen said.

'Maybe you need a glass of whiskey,' Owen said. 'Nothing like whiskey to perk up a person. I base that opinion on years of empirical research. Marcus, as a news-paperman, do you agree?'

'Those of us who profess to be newspapermen are known to have a drink or two.'

'Or three or four,' Owen said. 'How about it, Mrs Swearingen?'

'No, thank you.'

'Why don't you lie down?' Ezra asked. 'You need to get some rest.'

'Well, Mr McPherson,' Swearingen said. 'I appreciate the interest you show in my wife's well-being.'

She looked hard at her husband, and he smiled a smile that told her he knew. She wondered whether Ezra saw the smile, whether he understood.

'Ginevra, I care about your well-being also, just as much as Mr McPherson does, perhaps even more. Family is

99

important to me. Why do you think I've built this ranch? I didn't do it for myself. I did it for my family. Yes, there's nothing more important to me than family. And when someone has someone that belongs to me, I want him back.'

She wondered what he was leading to. He turned and faced Ezra.

'You and your friend Chesterfield and your new sheriff have something that is mine.'

'What are you talking about?' Ezra asked.

'This is no time for a disagreement,' Ginevra said. 'Anne has just given birth. Have you already forgotten?'

'There's no disagreement,' Swearingen said. 'In fact, I'm sure we're all in agreement – that what is mine is mine.'

'Well, hell, Swearingen,' Owen said, 'you don't hear us taking issue with what you're saying.'

'I think you need to be a bit more specific. What is your point?'

'You're holding my son in jail. I want him back. Do you understand?'

Ginevra rose.

'Andrew is in jail?'

'I'm not sure what you said to our son,' Swearingen said, 'but you certainly confused him. He has turned himself in to the sheriff. He is taking responsibility for something that was not his doing. Apparently you put some crazy ideas in his head. Anyway, I want him here with me. McPherson, I'll give you and Chesterfield and this newspaper dude time to get back to town and talk some sense into the new sheriff. This afternoon, if Andrew has not returned home, I'm going to come for him, and I won't come alone. Is that clear, McPherson? If blood in the streets of Cheyenne is what you want, then blood in the streets of Cheyenne is what you will have.'

Swearingen walked, heavy, out of the room. Ginevra looked at each of the men. Tears glistened in her dark eyes.

'Ezra, why didn't you tell me?'

'He was not in jail when we left,' Ezra said.

'That's the truth,' Owen said. 'I don't know what your husband is talking about.'

Ezra took her hand.

'We'll return to town,' he said. 'We'll find out what's going on.'

'Don't let anything happen to Andrew,' she said. 'Please, Ezra, I'm begging you. Richard is a violent man. To get what he wants, he's willing to do – just about anything.'

Ezra kissed her forehead gently.

'Marcus, pour me another whiskey,' Owen said. 'While you're at it, pour one for yourself. And then we have to go. Cheyenne awaits.'

Meta Anderson stood at the window. Dark figures squatted just beyond her mother's flower bed that bore no blooms. They had to be talking about something important. That was what her mother had always told her. You see men on their haunches, her mother had said, and you know they're talking about something important – at least they think it's important whether anyone else does or not. The men had ridden up and called out to her father. Jeremy Anderson and Lem Davis and her three brothers went outside, and they talked. They kept their voices quiet. The men were homesteaders. Her brothers squatted just behind them. They're trying to be men, she said to herself. They're so young, but they're trying real hard. The pine floor was warm, gritty beneath her bare feet.

Already the eastern sky above the dark hilltops reddened. Some of the men smoked, the tips of their cigarettes red like the sunrise. Some of the men chewed and spat. One of the men had a large knife. He dug the blade into the dust again and again.

'Meta, come back from the window,' her mother called from behind the curtain that separated her bed from the main room.

'I'm just listening.'

'It's not for you to eavesdrop, young lady.'

Her mother and Mrs Davis tiptoed next to her, as if the men could hear their approach. The man with the knife scooped up dust and flung it away from the group. Apparently he did not agree with something her father said.

'I know what you think of Andrew Swearingen,' her father said. 'I can't say I trust him myself, but there was something about him that makes me want to see how things turn out. I think we should wait.'

'Wait, hell, I'm tired of waiting,' one of the men said. 'Wait for them to come in the middle of the night and burn us out like they did to you, Davis? No, sir. I say we ride into Cheyenne and hang that young Swearingen buck. When I found out he was in jail, I said to myself, what an opportunity to serve justice, the only kind of justice men like Swearingen understand.'

'We shouldn't do something rash,' Davis said. 'I agree with Jeremy. I think we should wait. Let's see how the law handles this.'

'Law. What law? Harrison is dead. Do you think Zeke Stuart will know what to do? Anderson, he ain't much older than your boys.'

The men stood. They scraped their boots in the dirt, as if expecting to find an answer to their debate beneath them.

'Anderson, we all know that Swearingen and his men

will ride into town later today to get his son. If this law you have such faith in doesn't let him go, there's going to be a gun battle the likes of which Cheyenne hasn't seen in many a year. Zeke Stuart doesn't stand a chance going up against Swearingen and his men. Stuart will end up just like Harrison. And when that happens, Swearingen will send his boy back to New York and he'll never get what's coming to him.'

'We should let the law deal with it,' Anderson said.

'Damn, Anderson, you're hardheaded.'

'I just don't want unnecessary bloodshed. After talking with Andrew Swearingen, I am convinced he feels the same way. I don't believe he wants any more killing.'

'All right. Let's suppose we do as you suggest. We let the law handle this. Let's suppose Zeke Stuart prevails against the old man. And let's suppose the young Swearingen goes to trial. He deserves to be hanged, but there's not a jury in Wyoming that's going to sentence him to be hanged. He may get a prison sentence. He may just get a friendly slap on the wrist. But, Anderson, do you honestly think that will settle anything? If Andrew thinks his going to prison solves anything, he's naïve. We will still have what his old man wants – our land. His old man will fight to take it. We will fight to defend it. There's no getting around it. What you want us to do is simply to put off the inevitable. But rest assured – we can all put this in our pipes and smoke it – war is coming, and whatever happens to Andrew Swearingen is not going to prevent it.'

The farmers grunted and stood tall in the fading darkness. They stretched the soreness out of their joints and mounted their horses and rode off. Anderson and Davis and the three brothers walked inside the cabin.

'Well, did you hear?' Anderson asked.

'We heard enough,' his wife Isabelle said. 'I think we

might as well have some coffee.'

'No need to stop with coffee,' Anderson said. 'Bacon and eggs goes with coffee.'

Meta went onto the porch and stared in the direction of the riders. Then she stared at the black Wyoming sky as yet untouched by the redness in the east. How many stars are there, she wondered. I've never seen so many. John would say, 'What a sight'. Pans rattled and coffee perked. Her mother called for her, but she did not respond. She left the porch and walked to the barn.

She climbed the ladder and went to a bale of hay in a corner of the loft. She reached behind it. I've kept it hidden real good, she said to herself. No one has found it. Not Pa, not my brothers. She went back down the ladder and walked to the stall where the mule stood.

'Buttercup, are you ready to do some more traveling? Are you ready to go back to Cheyenne? I know you are. It's a good day to travel.'

Her mother called again.

CHAPTER TWELVE

'I'm going to walk Jennifer to the door,' Luke said.

'Mrs Beauchamp, where does Mr Taylor keep his buggy and horse?' Ezra asked.

'Out back in the barn.'

'I'll see to it. Owen, you and Stokesbury take the horses back to the livery. I'll meet up with you at the jail. I'll be along directly.'

Luke took Jennifer's hand and led her up the steps onto the porch. They were tired. Strands of blonde hair fell across her face, and she wiped them away.

'I'm sure I'm a terrible sight to behold,' she said.

'Jennifer, once again, I can't—'

'You have thanked me enough.'

She stood on her tiptoes and kissed him. She opened the door and went through the parlor to the kitchen. Charlotte stood at the sink washing dishes.

'How's mother and baby?' Charlotte asked.

'Fine. It's been quite an experience. How's Bobby?'

'He's fine too. He's back in his room going through a McGuffey Reader. You've taught him well.'

'Has Silas already gone to the store?'

'Oh, yes. Honey, you look plum worn out. Sit down and rest and tell me everything that happened.'

Ezra and Luke walked in the early morning heat past the small houses. Ezra knew Luke wanted to talk. It seemed the young man was fighting to keep the words penned in, but he was losing the fight.

'Ezra, I'm going to marry her.'

'I figured.'

'I'm going to stay.'

'I figured.'

'Have you ever considered expanding your vocabulary?'

'I say what needs to be said.'

'Father isn't going to be happy.'

'It's your decision, not his.'

'I never dreamed something like this would happen. She's wonderful, Ezra.'

'She's a nice young lady. Luke, I'm going to give you a piece of advice. I learned a long time ago that when you find the right woman, you'd better hold on to her. Don't let her get away.'

'I'm not going to. And I think Bobby likes me.'

'I think he does. The boy needs a father. You'll make a good one.'

Ezra slowed his pace.

'Ezra, is everything all right?'

'Back at the Swearingen ranch, while you were outside with Mrs Beauchamp, Swearingen told us his son Andrew is in jail. He's turned himself in. I've got to get to the bottom of this. There's going to be trouble. No getting around it. If we don't release Andrew, if we don't persuade Andrew that he needs to leave – that sounds a bit strange, doesn't it? – Swearingen will come for him. He told Owen and me that's what he's going to do. I'm sure he's got a passel of hired guns, and these men won't be like the ones who tried to rob the train. Luke, men are going to die. I don't want you to be one of them. I want you to stay clear of any shooting. I promised your father I'd watch out for you. I haven't forgotten my responsibility.'

'That sounds like a lot of exaggeration. I doubt things will be that bad.'

'I've found that violence is like a wind storm, the kind that rushes in from the northwest in the dead of winter. There's no turning it back. It just has to blow itself out.'

Eloise Endicott stepped outside her office and admired the sunlit morning. In her hand she held a notepad and pencil. She headed toward the jail. Outside the general store Silas Taylor swept. Like the other shopkeepers, he did the same thing every morning. Getting rid of the dust was impossible. Still, he swept. His face was red. His white shirt was already wet.

'Have you had any word from the Swearingen ranch?' she asked.

'No, ma'am, not a word.'

'Well, this is Anne Swearingen's first. Sometimes the first ones take their time.'

As soon as she said it, she wished she hadn't. The Taylors had lost their first and only one in childbirth.

'I'm sorry. I shouldn't—'

'No need to apologize. The dark blue of your dress looks really good. That reminds me – some new catalogues have come in, two from New York, one from Paris. When you have a moment, I'd like to show them to you.'

'I will – later this week.'

'You know, I think Doctor Tisdale is pretty sweet on Jennifer, but don't print it.'

'Is she sweet on him?'

He smiled and she crossed the almost deserted street and entered the jail. Zeke Stuart sat behind the desk. He stood. The glare from the open door almost blinded him.

'Did you get any sleep last night?' she asked.

'Not much. There was trouble at the Two Rivers.'

'What kind of trouble?'

'Rose, one of the girls that work at the Two Rivers, shot herself.'

Eloise imagined that Lawrence Byrd already knew. He was probably already writing the article.

'How is your prisoner?'

'He's all right, I guess. He didn't eat much breakfast. He doesn't say much. He just stares at the wall.'

'May I talk to him?'

Stuart hesitated.

'About what?'

'He's news. I need to put in my story what he has to say. I promise I won't try to help him escape.'

'Escape is not on his mind.'

'Well?'

'I don't see that it'd do any harm. But he may not want to talk.'

'If he doesn't want to talk, then I'll put that in the story.'

Stuart opened the heavy wooden door and she walked into the cell block. Andrew stood next to the back wall.

'I'm Eloise Endicott. I was here last night when you came in.'

'I remember.'

'I'm the editor of the newspaper.'

'I know who you are.'

'I'd like to ask you some questions.'

'I don't want to talk. Not now anyway.'

'I want to ask you some questions about Cliff Darton's lynching.'

'Ma'am, you need to leave.'

'What made you decide to turn yourself in?'

'I had to.'

'What made you think you had to?'

'I just did.'

'Do you think you should hang for what you did?'

'That's not for me to decide.'

'Does your father know you're here?'

'I reckon he'll know soon enough. I'm not answering any more questions.'

Stuart leaned back in the chair behind the desk. The idea of deputizing Ezra McPherson and Owen Chesterfield at first did not appeal to him, but now he wished they would come back. Andrew Swearingen behind bars. Of his own volition. Stuart still couldn't believe it. Old man Swearingen will come for him, Stuart thought. He'll probably ride into town with an army of men, trained killers.

Eloise emerged from the cell block. She looked at her notepad and shook her head.

'I guess you've got a story for the next edition,' he said.

'I was hoping to get more out of him. He doesn't want to talk. Something's happened to him. I can't quite put my finger on it, but he just doesn't seem like the Andrew Swearingen the town has come to love and admire.'

'I guess killing does something to a man,' Stuart said. 'I'm sure he learned how to shoot by blasting tin cans off a fence post. That's how I learned. But tin cans don't shoot back. And when you hit them, they don't bleed. He learned that in the Two Rivers.'

Eloise walked onto the sidewalk. Marcus and Owen were crossing the street.

'I can take one quick look at you gents and tell you didn't get much sleep last night. How's Anne Swearingen? How's the baby?'

'Both are doing well,' Marcus said.

'That baby took his time, but Luke did a fine job.'

'That's good news. I'll print something about it. I guess

you've heard about Andrew Swearingen.'

'Yes, ma'am, we have,' Owen said. 'It came as a surprise.'

'I'm sure it did. Where are Ezra and Doctor Tisdale?'

'They'll be along directly,' Owen said.

'Would you like me to have somebody bring breakfast for you?'

'Ma'am, not only are you a newspaper publisher,' Owen said, 'but you're an angel. We ate a long time ago. Riding across the Wyoming prairie builds up an appetite.'

She walked toward Lou's Restaurant across from the hotel. Shoppers – and there were not many early in the morning – smiled and went in and out of the stores. Everything seemed normal, yet something was different. She felt uneasy.

She stopped at the playhouse. Playbills announcing the upcoming performance of *Hamlet* were nailed to the wall on either side of the door. The troupe had performed in New York, Boston, Philadelphia, and Chicago. And now they were in Cheyenne. 'We've gotten culture,' she said. 'We're not the West we once were.'

Even as she said it, she did not believe it. And she thought about Hamlet and old Hamlet and Hamlet's uncle and Hamlet's mother. She thought about the rottenness. Yes, she said to herself, there was rottenness in Denmark. And she looked up and down the street. Benjamin Payne stood outside his clothing store. Even though he was across the street, she could see the concern on his face. He probably wished he was not the mayor. Yes, there was rottenness, and he did not know how to deal with it. He raised his hand, but she did not return the greeting.

'No, we're not the West we once were,' she said again. 'We're not. There has to be an end to the killing. There simply has to be.'

She continued toward the restaurant. She kept telling herself that Cheyenne had changed.

CHAPTER THIRTEEN

Ezra stood outside the jail cell and stared. Andrew sat on his cot. He looked small, vulnerable.

'Look at me,' Ezra said.

'I don't know why you're here.'

'That's what I should be saying. Didn't your mother tell you to get far away from Cheyenne?'

'My mother—'

'Andrew, why did you come back?'

'I had to. I couldn't run. What I did was wrong. I can't run from it.'

'What you've done will get more men killed.'

'I came back to prevent more men from being killed.'

'Well, I reckon we'll see soon enough who's right.'

Ezra closed the door and sat in one of the straight chairs near Stuart's desk. Luke, Marcus, and Owen sat next to the far wall.

'Swearingen is going to come for him,' Ezra said.

'I figured he would,' Stuart said.

'You fellows need to get some rest,' Owen said.

'You do, too,' Stokesbury said.

'I'm all right. I've gone without sleep plenty of times before,' Ezra said.

'Yeah, but you're not as young as you used to be,' Owen said.

'When do you think Swearingen will come?' Stuart asked.

'This afternoon. He'll wait to see if Andrew returns.'

'Why don't we move Andrew to another town?' Luke said.

'Swearingen and his men would probably catch up with us. If we're going to deal with them, I'd rather do it here than in the middle of the prairie.'

'Just unlock the door and throw him out into the street,' Luke said.

'I wish we could,' Ezra said, 'but he's confessed to a crime. We have to keep him. A judge and jury will decide what to do with him.'

'This is one hell of a mess,' Owen said. 'Maybe Swearingen will decide not to come. After all, he's got a new grandbaby.'

'Do you believe that?'

'No.'

'Luke, why don't you go to the hotel? There's nothing for you to do here.'

'I want to stay.'

'Suit yourself. But when Swearingen comes, you stay in here. No matter what happens, don't go into the street. Stokesbury, this is not your fight. You're a newspaperman, not a lawman. I'll say the same thing to you that I said to Luke. Go to the hotel – or go to Miss Endicott's newspaper. You don't belong here.'

'You're wrong, Ezra. I do belong here. You're going to need all the help you can get.'

'What kind of help can you give?'

'I've fired a shotgun and rifle a time or two.'

'At a man who's firing back at you? Go see Miss Endicott.'

'I'm staying here.'

'There's a shotgun in the rack on the wall. When the time comes, if you insist on standing with us, I want you to take it. We'll do everything we can to prevent a shootout. But if shooting starts, aim at somebody who's firing at us. With a twelve-gauge, you're bound to hit something. I just hope it's not one of us.'

The afternoon hours crawled. The heat was relentless. Shadows inched their way across the floor. Stuart lay on a cot in one of the cells. Owen sat in a chair, his head tilted, and snored. Luke read the most recent copy of the *Cheyenne Daily Times*. Marcus said he needed some air, but Ezra knew what he was doing. He was going to keep an eye out for Swearingen.

At the end of the lower veranda, Swearingen admired the barn, the corral, the bunk houses. All this is mine, he thought. I've built it from nothing. And it's going to be Andrew's. This is not the kind of life Peter wants. But Andrew is cut out for it. Nobody is going to interfere. Not Ginevra, not Zeke Stuart, not McPherson.

McPherson.

I know, I know, I know. You may think I don't, but I do. You and Ginevra. I've seen the way you look at each other. I saw how concerned you were about her. It was touching. Damn touching. I thought I was going to cry. She's the one who's going to cry – when your worthless body is buried beneath this merciless Wyoming sun.

Two ranch hands walked past the veranda and tipped their hats.

'Afternoon, Mr Swearingen.'

'Afternoon, boys. Don't let this heat get you down.'

'No, sir. We're managing.'

'Let us know when you want us to teach that baby how

114

to lasso a calf.'

'You betcha. Maybe next week. I have to tell you – that baby is going to be as ornery as his grandpa.'

The men laughed and made their way toward the corral. Peter came onto the porch and lit a cigarette.

'Want one?' Peter asked.

'Sure. Why not? How's Anne?'

'Sleeping. She's doing fine. Doctor Tisdale did a good job.'

'Yeah, he did a good job. Like his brother, he's a professional.'

'You miss John, don't you?'

'Yes, I do. He was a fine lawyer. More than that, he was a fine man. We didn't always see eye to eye on some things, but I always respected his opinion. I hope we catch the scoundrel who killed him.'

'Is there much chance of that happening?'

'I'm afraid not.'

'Father, I was talking with Mother. She's in the parlor. She can't sleep. She told me about Andrew.'

'It's quite a surprise, isn't it? Life's full of surprises. I should know by now. Who would have thought Andrew would get it in his head to go to jail? What kind of a fool thing was that to do?'

'I wish I could say Andrew and I are close, but we're not. He doesn't confide a whole lot to me. But maybe if I ride into town and talk to him and talk to the sheriff, I can straighten this thing out.'

'I'm afraid it's beyond straightening out.'

For Swearingen the cigarette was good. It eased his mind.

'I don't understand.'

'Some of us are going to ride into Cheyenne and bring Andrew back. He's just a little confused. Something has gotten into his head. That doesn't mean he belongs in jail. Hell, half the country is confused. The Congress of the United States of America is confused. What are we going to do? Put handcuffs on all of them? No, sir. Being confused is not a crime. Andrew should not be in jail. He should be here. If the law doesn't see it my way, then I'll deal with them accordingly.'

Peter realized his father was wearing a gun belt.

'I've never seen you carry a pistol.'

'Sometimes situations demand that we carry one.'

'Father, don't cause trouble. I know this business with Andrew can be worked out without violence. Obviously Andrew went to jail because he thought it was something he needed to do. We have to respect that.'

'You think I'm the cause of his problems, don't you?'

'I didn't say that.'

'But it's what you think.'

'Father, like I said, Andrew doesn't confide in me, nor do you. I'm an outsider in this family. I don't know the extent of my brother's problems, and I don't know their cause.'

'Well, you know business. You know the ins and outs of finance. I've never told you this, Peter, but you know more about finance than I do. No matter what happens today, the firm back in New York is yours to run.'

'Don't talk like that. Go inside. See Mother. She needs you.'

'She doesn't need me. She needs comforting from someone else.'

Peter did not understand, but he knew asking questions would clarify little. He finished the cigarette and went back inside.

Rayburn leaned against the front wall of the bunkhouse. He stared at the large house with the double verandas, and he wondered what Swearingen and his older son could be talking about. The old man had never had much to say to the boy, so why was he talking to him now?

Rayburn went inside the dark bunkhouse. Already Simmons, Bradford, Weekes, and Gilman were in their chaps. Simmons and Bradford were from Texas, Weekes from Nevada, and nobody knew where Gilman was from. That was something he never talked about. They were good, highly recommended, more proficient than the men who tried to rob the train. Rayburn knew their previous bosses. Their opinions meant something.

And then there was Treutlin. He was the youngest of the bunch, but also the fastest. Perhaps a little too confident.

'So we're breaking Andrew out of jail,' Weekes said.

'It may not come to that,' Rayburn said.

'I haven't broke anybody out of jail since I was in Arizona,' Bradford said. 'I went to a passel of trouble to do it. When we were hightailin' it out of town, somebody shot him in the back. All that trouble – nothing to show for it.'

'Is it true that fellow McPherson is a deputy?' Simmons asked.

'McPherson?' Gilman echoed. 'Are we going up against him?'

'What's the matter, Gilman?' Treutlin asked. 'Are you afraid? McPherson is getting up in years. Just leave him to me.'

'We're paying you men to follow orders,' Rayburn said. 'If you're afraid, then you can get the hell out of here.'

'We ain't afraid.'

'Nobody said anything about being afraid.'

'It's just Treutlin running his mouth.'

'Yeah, his mouth is going to get him in trouble.'

'That's enough,' Rayburn said. 'Go to the barn and saddle up. Saddle Swearingen's horse too.'

Rayburn left the bunkhouse and walked up to the big house. He saw the gun belt.

'It looks like you're prepared for trouble.'

'It's best to be prepared.'

'There's no sign of Andrew.'

'Then it's time to ride into Cheyenne and fetch him home. Have you picked out reliable men?'

'Indeed I have. They've got your horse ready.'

Swearingen and Rayburn joined the others in the barn, and they rode down the drive in the bright afternoon sunlight. From a window in the parlor Peter watched. Ginevra came into the room.

'What are you watching so intently?'

'Father is riding into Cheyenne. He's going to try to bring Andrew home.'

'He doesn't know what he's doing.'

'He thinks he does.'

'He's never encountered a man like Ezra McPherson.'

'You sound as if you know him well.'

'Have someone saddle my horse.'

'Surely you're not—'

'Just do as I say.'

CHAPTER FOURTEEN

Ezra heard the footsteps before the door knob turned. The footsteps were light, so he was not concerned. Still, he put his pistol on top of the desk. His hand rested on the grip.

Eloise walked in. Ezra had never looked at a magazine devoted to the latest fashions. Somehow he suspected that if he were to look at a copy, he would probably find a blue silk dress like the one she wore. He had to admit she was lovely, and for a moment he wondered why a woman as lovely as her was not married. Well, it's none of my business, he said to himself.

'Owen knows how to snore,' she said. 'Where are the others?'

'Zeke is asleep. Luke was reading your newspaper. It made him sleepy, so he's on a cot in one of the cells.'

'If my newspaper makes readers sleepy, I've got work to do. Where's Marcus?'

'Stretching his legs.'

'Aren't you tired?'

'Yes.'

She sat and picked up the newspaper and fanned herself.

'This is some of the worst heat we've had,' she said. 'How can you stay in this jail? It's suffocating.'

'You get used to it.'

'Nothing seems to bother you.'

'Interviews bother me.'

'I'm not going to interview you. Don't worry. By the way, I'll have supper brought to you men.'

'That's not necessary. You had breakfast brought over.'

'It's something I want to do.'

'Well, thank you. But there may not be an opportunity to eat supper.'

'You can ask Swearingen not to cause any trouble until after you've eaten your supper.'

'I'm sure he'd be willing to accommodate.'

'Ezra, I have to ask a question – and, no, I'm not interviewing you. What do you think Jesse would say if he were alive and if he knew you're wearing a deputy's badge?'

'I haven't given any thought to it.'

'Give some thought to it. What would he say?'

'It wouldn't be something you could print in your newspaper. And then he'd probably try to kill me.'

'But he wouldn't be successful.'

'No, of course not. I'd kill him first.'

'All this talk of killing. There's no end to it, is there?'

'Sure doesn't look that way.'

Stuart opened the door and left the cell block and rubbed his eyes and walked past Owen. Ezra stood.

'This chair is yours,' Ezra said.

'No, you keep it. You look more at home in it than I do. I've been awake for a while. I heard talk about Jesse. Did you know Jesse James?'

I should not have let Zeke know, Eloise said to herself. I should not have asked the question.

'I'm going back to the newspaper,' she said. 'I've done

120

enough damage here.'

She left and Stuart approached the desk.

'Did you know him?'

'I knew him.'

'Did he rob you? Maybe you were in a bank when he robbed it.'

'Not exactly.'

'You rode with him, didn't you?'

'Yes.'

'Why didn't you tell me?'

'There was no need.'

'How many men have you killed?'

'I don't know. The number doesn't matter.'

'Are you wanted?'

'Yes, he is,' Owen said, and he yawned and tried to shake off his sleep. 'I was having a pleasant dream, and you gentlemen woke me up. Yes, Ezra McPherson is wanted, but not by the law. He's wanted by a lot of young cowpokes who want to make a name by gunning down Ezra McPherson, but we're not going to let that happen, are we, Zeke?'

'No, we're not. Sheriff Harrison told me you were the past come to Cheyenne.'

'I reckon he was right,' Ezra said.

'I don't care if you did ride with Jesse James. I appreciate what you're doing. I don't think I could go through this by myself.'

'You'll be all right,' Owen said.

'I've never shot at a man before. If we face off against Swearingen and his hired guns, I don't know how I'll react. Maybe I'll run.'

'Well, if you do,' Owen said, 'I'll shoot you in your rear end.'

'He's not joking,' Ezra said. 'So you'd better not run. Don't worry, Zeke. When the time comes, you'll do the right thing.'

Stuart tried to give the impression he was a man. That was especially true at the meeting of the town council. Sometimes, though, he felt like a boy. This was one of those times. He felt like a boy who wanted to hear tales of the West.

'What was Jesse James like?' Stuart asked.

Ezra found it difficult to talk about Jesse and Frank James. He preferred to keep what he knew bottled up, but somehow this moment was different. He could not explain why.

'At first he was a friend, the closest friend I had except for his brother, Frank. He was brave, one of the bravest men I've ever known. He was fierce. But the war – the killing – did something to him. Killing will do terrible things to a man.'

'I hope you don't mind my asking, but when did you kill your first man?'

Ezra remembered. It was during the war. The town was small. He never knew if it even had a name. All he knew was that it was in Kansas. They just wanted to scare the folks a bit, to make sure they didn't help the Yankees. Jesse said it would be fun. Frank thought it would be a waste of bullets.

'How 'bout you, Ezra?' Jesse asked. 'What do you think?'

'I don't see the point.'

'Hell, it's war. There's no point to anything.'

So they rode up and down the street, yelling and firing into the air. It was the middle of the day, and women and children screamed and ran inside buildings. And then there was the man with a rifle. It looked like a musket, long and old. Jesse didn't see him. The man wore an apron, bloodied from meat he obviously had been cutting for a customer. He took aim at Jesse's back, and Ezra shouted and fired before the man pulled the trigger. The bullet struck the man in the middle of his chest and he fell. Suddenly a boy, no older than Bobby Beauchamp, was kneeling beside the man.

'Pa! Pa! Say something, Pa! Don't die, Pa!'

Ezra jumped from his horse and ran to the boy.

'You killed my pa! You killed my pa!'

The boy was crying. The front of the man's shirt was soaked in red. There was nothing Ezra could do.

'I'm sorry. I'm – so – sorry.'

'Ezra saved your life, Jesse,' Frank said.

'Much obliged, Ezra. Come on. Let's get going.'

Ezra did not want to leave the boy, but he did. He mounted his horse and rode after the others.

Few were the times when Ezra had cried. But on that day, as he rode out of town, he wept. The past haunted his memories.

'Zeke, maybe we shouldn't ask things like that,' Owen said. 'We've got trouble coming our way. Let's focus on that.'

Ezra held his Colt firmly in his hand and checked the cylinder. Click, click, click. The sound was smooth. Stuart wanted to ask how many gunfights the Colt had seen – he saw that the dark brown handle was smooth – but he heeded Owen's advice. He remained quiet.

'Miss Endicott, is there anything else you want us to do? Do you want us to stay?'

Ingrid was one of the farm girls who worked on the newspaper in the afternoons. She and the others were hard workers. They learned quickly. Perhaps one day one of them, perhaps Ingrid, would publish a newspaper. It's a new day, Eloise thought.

'No, we've done enough for now. If you can come back later this evening, that would be good. We'll have a lot of work to do.'

'Yes, ma'am.'

Ingrid's family had come from Georgia.

'Ingrid, I know someone from Atlanta.'

'You do? I'm from a town called Marietta, just to the northwest of Atlanta.'

'He's a newspaperman. He has printer's ink in his veins just as we do.'

'I'd like to meet him.'

'He's in Cheyenne for a short while. Perhaps you will. And, Ingrid, I need to tell you something. For the next few hours, you and the other girls should stay off the street.'

'Is something wrong?'

'There may be trouble, and I don't want any of you to get hurt. You're welcome to stay here.'

Ingrid went to the back door, which opened into the room where the press sat ready to print. She stopped in a shaft of sunlight that fell through the window. Her light brown hair appeared even lighter.

'Will you be all right?' the girl asked.

'Yes, I'll be fine. Don't worry about me. Tell the girls what I said.'

'Yes, ma'am, I will.'

Eloise was so hot she felt faint. She opened the front door and stepped onto the sidewalk. Late afternoon shadows crept from the buildings across the street. Shoppers, for the most part, had left. Shopkeepers began to close their doors for the evening. At the end of the sidewalk, just inside the alley that ran alongside the newspaper office, Marcus stood. She walked toward him.

'Marcus, what on earth are you doing?'

'I have a good view of the livery from here.'

'I see. Was this Ezra's idea?'

'No, it was mine. When Swearingen rides into town, we need to know how many men he's bringing.'

'Will it make a difference?'

'Maybe. Maybe not.'

'Marcus, you're a newspaperman. You're not cut out for this sort of thing.'

'Ezra is going to need help. I'm going to do what I can.'

'You may get killed. Have you thought about that?'

'Yes, I have.'

'Then you're awfully brave, braver than I am.'

'You're the brave one, Eloise.'

'I've never thought of myself as brave. What have I done to be brave?'

'You publish a newspaper. It's not an easy task. With each issue you run the risk of making someone angry. Like any good publisher, you pursue the truth with a relentless passion. It doesn't matter if someone gets angry. I admire you.'

'Thank you, Marcus. You should consider publishing a newspaper yourself. You're not going to stay at the *Constitution* forever, are you?'

Marcus leaned against the side of the building and rubbed the toe of his brown shoe in the dust.

'I love Atlanta. I love the *Constitution*.'

'I can tell that you do.'

'I'm eager to get back. Me – an editor and publisher. That's an interesting idea. In northwest Georgia there's a small town called Kingston.'

'I haven't heard of it.'

'It's between Cartersville and Rome. I grew up there.'

'I've heard of Rome.'

'Kingston has a small paper. I've known the publisher all my life. He's an old man named Meade. I told him one day the only other Meade I was aware of was a Yankee general. I thought he was going to fight me. Apparently he didn't like his name being associated with a Yankee. When he calmed down, he told me he was thinking about selling. He told me this only about a year ago. He told me he would sell it to me. I've saved a little money. Kingston is a wonderful little town. Wonderful farming people. Ezra hunts quail on Jekyll Island. He should see the quail we have outside Kingston. When I was young, I was eager to leave Kingston, but I can see myself going back, settling down, and publishing the paper.'

'You should do it. There's nothing like having your own newspaper.'

'But first I have to return to the *Constitution*. My editor is expecting a story based on my adventures in Cheyenne.'

'I can't wait to read it.'

'You've never told me how you got into the newspaper business.'

'Marcus, I was born into the newspaper business. My father published a paper in Baltimore. My mother died when I was young. Dad kept me at the paper. I'm sure I often got in the way, but nobody seemed to mind. When I got older, I learned how to set type. I proofread. I sold advertising. I thought that Dad would, at some point, turn over the reins of the paper to me. But he said that, before I ran a big city paper, I needed to run a smalltown paper. So I ended up here in Cheyenne.'

'Do you plan to return to Baltimore?'

'Like your friend, Meade, Dad is getting up in years. Yes, I plan to return. But it will be hard leaving Cheyenne. I've come to love this town. It's still raw around the edges, but it has so much promise.'

'Perhaps you'll turn it over to Lawrence Byrd.'

'I've thought about it. But I don't think Cheyenne can

keep him. He's a talented writer. He knows how to dig for a story. He'll probably leave before I do. Marcus, do you have a cigarette? And don't get a funny look on your face. It is permissible for a woman to smoke if she wants to.'

He reached into his coat pocket and handed one to her. He struck a match and lit it.

'I would suggest that you come inside and have a glass of bourbon,' she said, 'but I guess that's something you don't want to do.'

'No, but thanks. I need to stay alert. You see, I've never done this sort of thing before.'

'I guess some men get used to it. I don't see how. Ezra is obviously used to it.'

'It's not something he enjoys.'

'No, it's not. That's why he left the James gang. He was tired of all the killing. It's possible that he, too, wants to settle down . . . with the woman he loves. The woman he loves, I believe, is Ginevra Swearingen.'

'Why do you say that?'

'When we had dinner at the Swearingen ranch, I saw the way they looked at each other. They knew each other. When I did some research on Ezra, more than one person in Missouri told me that they were lovers. For a time he was unwilling to leave Jesse. He wouldn't give up the life he was living. She considered it no life at all and she left.'

'That was a long time ago.'

'Love is not measured in time.'

Marcus turned his attention from the livery to Eloise. She stared across the street but it seemed to Marcus that she really was not looking at anything. Her thoughts had left Cheyenne and for the first time he realized that she cared about Ezra. She inhaled the smoke and released it.

Riders appeared at a darkened bend in the street well beyond the livery. They rode slowly. The man in the middle was large, as large as a gray granite boulder that had tumbled down a mountainside. Marcus knew at once that it was Swearingen. He counted the others.

'He's got six gunmen with him,' Marcus said.

'Maybe they're not all gunmen.'

'Rest assured, they are.'

The horsemen grew larger as they rode down the street. They passed the gentlemen's club and Marcus found it interesting that Swearingen stopped for only a moment and glanced over his shoulder at the building.

'The man next to Swearingen is Rayburn, the foreman,' Eloise said. 'He's a killer. I'm sure that's the reason Swearingen hired him. From what I've learned, Rayburn has wanted to kill Ezra for a long time. This is his chance.'

'Well, he's ridden a long way for nothing. I have to go back to the jail. Eloise, go into your office and stay there.'

'Marcus, please be careful. Remember your dream that is in Kingston. Don't let it die here in Cheyenne.'

CHAPTER FIFTEEN

Smitty struggled to pull open the corral gate and Swearingen and his men led their horses in. They said nothing. Smitty saw the determination. He saw the fury in Swearingen's face. He recognized Rayburn and Treutlin but not the others. He knew the kind of men Rayburn was hiring. They were not just cowpokes drifting from one ranch to the other. But in their eyes uncertainty shone, and Smitty found it interesting. These men are killers, hired guns, he said to himself. Why should they appear uncertain? Perhaps they had heard they would be facing Ezra McPherson. They had probably never met him, never even seen him. But they had heard about him. They had heard how Ezra stopped a train robbery and killed most of the robbers. They had heard how fast he was with a Colt. That would be enough to make anyone uncertain. The smell of death clung to them.

'We won't be long,' Swearingen said.

'I'm not going anywhere.'

'We have some business to attend to. Then we'll be back. Do you have Andrew's horse here?'

If your business involves Ezra McPherson, then you may not be back, Smitty wanted to say.

'Yes, sir, Mr Swearingen. I've got her.'

'Go ahead and saddle her.'

'Whatever you say, Mr Swearingen.'

The men stepped into the street. The loud whistle announced the arrival of the westbound train. Swearingen checked his gold pocket watch and returned it to his vest pocket. The street was empty. The sidewalk was empty. Everybody has heard we're coming, Swearingen thought. Well, they've done the smart thing. They've gotten out of the way. He wondered where the sheriff would confront them. Perhaps in the middle of the street. Perhaps at the jailhouse steps. We'll find out soon enough, he thought. Of course, what does it matter?

'I want it understood,' he said, 'there's to be no shooting unless it's called for.'

Rayburn checked the cylinder of his Colt. The other men did the same.

'They're not going to just hand Andrew over,' Rayburn said. 'If you want your son, you're going to have to fight. They'll fight to keep him.'

'You heard what I said. If it comes to a fight, then we'll fight, but only if it's necessary. When they see how serious we are, I figure they'll let him go. There's no point in a bunch of men getting shot up. We don't have far to walk. I'm not going to stand here all evening talking about it.'

'You're the boss.'

Jennifer and Charlotte sat on the sofa in the small parlor and sipped coffee. Bobby was playing in the back yard, probably climbing a tree. Jennifer had tried to discourage him. She had warned him he might fall and break an arm, but he was too much like his father. He was going to do what he wanted to do.

'I've always liked a cup of coffee late in the afternoon,' Charlotte said. 'There's just something about it that's soothing.'

'I'm sure you need something soothing after putting up with Bobby and me all day.'

'It's wonderful having both of you here. I can't tell you how good it is to have a child running in and out of the house.'

'You and Silas have been so good. At some point, though, I'm going to have to find a place for us. I don't want us to become a nuisance.'

'Nonsense. You're not a nuisance. I'm awfully proud of you.'

'Why?'

'What you did last night – helping Doctor Tisdale deliver the baby.'

'I'm just glad I was able to help.'

'You and Doctor Tisdale must work well together.'

Jennifer shrugged her shoulders.

'You're not fooling me, young lady,' Charlotte said.

The door opened and Silas walked in. Charlotte was surprised. She could not remember a day when he came home from the store this early. She looked at his face and knew something was wrong.

'What is it, Silas?'

He dropped into the rocking chair near the fireplace. His face was red. Back and forth he rocked. He did not want to upset them. Damn, he thought, there's no getting around it. The best thing is to go ahead and tell them.

'Old Mose Kittner came into the store a little while ago. You know how he is when he gets excited.'

'Yes, he flaps his arms around like he's going to take flight, and he stutters so much I can hardly understand a word he says. Why did he go into the store?'

'I guess all the other stores had already closed. He told me Swearingen was riding into town with an army. He said there was going to be trouble. I decided to do what everybody else apparently had done. I closed the store and came on home.'

'What kind of trouble?' Jennifer asked.

'Swearingen's youngest son, Andrew, is in jail. It's a strange thing. Word has it that he turned himself in to the new sheriff. He's taking responsibility for a lynching. I don't know too many of the details. Mose said the old man is coming to get him. Swearingen expects Zeke Stuart to release him. I don't see how that can happen. It seems to me that Judge Henry will have to decide whether he stands trial.'

'You know how Mose exaggerates,' Charlotte said.

'I doubt that Swearingen is bringing an army,' Silas said. 'I'm sure that's one of Mose's exaggerations. But I have a feeling Swearingen is coming, and I'm sure he will bring some help.'

'I have to go,' Jennifer said. 'Luke is in town.'

'You shouldn't go into town, Jennifer,' Silas said. 'If there is trouble – and there may not be any – you don't want to get caught up in it. I'm sure Doctor Tisdale will be fine. Stay here. That's what he would want you to do.'

'I must go.'

'Silas is right,' Charlotte said. 'You should stay here. There's nothing you can do right now. Besides, there's Bobby.'

'There'll probably be a whole lot of talking, a whole lot of cursing that a young lady should not hear,' Silas said. 'When they let out all their steam, they'll be tired. Swearingen will most likely listen to reason and he'll go back home. Then you can go into town. Invite Doctor Tisdale for supper. I'm sure Charlotte is planning one of her delicious meals. We can sit around the table and laugh about how worried we all were for no reason.'

Jennifer went to the back door and saw Bobby. He was crouched on a lower tree branch next to the trunk. He held a long piece of wood that Silas had helped him carve into the shape of a rifle. It didn't look much like a rifle, but for Bobby it was close enough. He balanced on the branch and aimed the rifle and shouted, 'Bang!' He lowered the rifle and inspected the terrain. Apparently more bad guys were approaching. Quickly he raised the rifle and fired several shots and Jennifer turned away.

She went into her bedroom and sat on the edge of the bed. The curtains blocked the dying sunlight. She bowed her head and prayed.

Marcus ran to the jail. Ezra and Owen knew immediately that Swearingen was in town. Stuart wiped the sweat from his face with a red bandana. He felt faint. He wanted to get some fresh air.

'How many are there?' Ezra asked.

'There's Swearingen and six others. I was talking with Eloise when they rode into town. She said one of the men is the foreman, a man named Rayburn.'

Luke left the cell block and joined them.

'I can't believe I've slept all afternoon.'

'What's Andrew doing?' Stuart asked.

'He's just sitting on his cot, staring at the floor. I spoke to him, but he didn't say anything. I don't believe he even heard me.'

'His old man has just ridden into town,' Ezra said. 'We're going to have a little talk with him – out in the street. You stay here.'

'You may have to patch up a few folks when this is all over,' Owen said. 'I just hope it's not any of us.'

Ezra handed the twelve-gauge shotgun to Marcus.

'Do you still want to come with us?'

Marcus took the shotgun.

'Put these extra shells in your coat pocket,' Ezra said.

The front door swung open and Curly Pike walked in.

'Curly, what are you doing here?' Stuart asked.

'I thought you might need some help. I'm pretty good with a gun. I ain't an expert like you gents, but I do all right.'

Stuart looked at Ezra.

'Your employer may not appreciate you taking shots at him,' Ezra said.

'He ain't my employer no more. He has hired guns. They're good. They mean business.'

'I don't understand why you want to help us,' Stuart said.

'A man like Swearingen has gotta be stopped. There's been too much bloodshed already. I want law and order as much as the next man. If you have another gun, maybe him and his men will back down.'

'We're trying to avoid bloodshed. All right. You can stand with us. Just don't do anything foolish. It's getting as crowded in here as the church on Sunday.'

'Well, this is where all the lost souls congregate,' Owen said.

Ezra kept his eye on Curly. Something about him seemed a bit strange. There was something not quite right, and he didn't know what it was. Ezra walked onto the sidewalk and looked up the street. Swearingen marched past the newspaper office. Rayburn and Treutlin and four others followed. Their stride was firm, confident. He went back inside.

'They're here,' Ezra said.

Each man looked at Stuart. Well, this is what the town is paying me to do, he said to himself. He took one quick glance at the empty chair behind the desk. He wanted to see Harrison sitting there.

'I'll go first,' Stuart said.

Stuart took a deep breath and led the men through the door. One by one they stepped into the street, into the pale sunlight of the late Wyoming afternoon. It had been a long time since Marcus walked the fields alongside the Etowah River near Kingston and hunted quail, a long time since he last held a shotgun. It felt heavy, heavier than he remembered. The extra shells bulged in his coat pocket.

On either side of Stuart walked Ezra and Owen. Next to Owen was Marcus. Next to Ezra was Curly. The street was deserted. At the front window of the jail Luke stood. His heart was racing.

'Is anybody out there?' Andrew called.

'Yes, I'm here. Luke Tisdale.'

'Doctor Tisdale, please come here.'

Luke went to the cell. Andrew clutched the bars of the cell door.

'Let me go talk to my father.'

'I think it best if we let the sheriff handle things.'

'Zeke doesn't know him. Men are going to die. Please let me try to put a stop to it. I've already got enough blood on my hands. Please, Doctor Tisdale, let me try.'

Luke did not know what to do. Andrew seemed sincere enough. In fact, he looked desperate. He gripped the bars so tightly that his knuckles were white. Luke was certain Ezra would tell him to keep Andrew in the cell, but perhaps Andrew could do some good. Perhaps it would be worth a try. Luke hurried to the sheriff's desk and opened each drawer until he found the key. Then he unlocked the cell door.

The two groups of men stopped about twenty feet from each other. Suddenly Benjamin Payne was in the middle of the street. He had walked from his haberdashery. He looked first at Stuart, then at Swearingen.

'Gentlemen.'

He expected an immediate response, but there was only silence. It was almost as if they did not see him.

'Gentlemen.'

'This is no time for speech making,' Swearingen said.

Payne was nervous. He had to say something to stop what he was certain was about to happen. They don't want to listen, he thought. They've gone mad, all of them.

'I'm not going to make a speech.'

'Then get out of the way.'

'I'm not going to make a speech, but I do have something to say. Gentlemen, think about what you're doing to our town. Think about the image we have cultivated. Think about what you're doing to it. We want more business to come here. In a few minutes the street lights are going to shine. Electric street lights. That's the kind of town we live in. The days of gunfights in the streets are over.'

'I thought you said you weren't going to make a speech,' Rayburn said.

'You men are trying to turn back the clock. You can't do that. You've got to look to the future. These street lights are just the beginning of what is to come. Bloodshed will put an abrupt stop to progress. Investors will not want to put their money in a place where men are shot down in the middle of the street. Surely, Mr Swearingen, you can appreciate what I'm saying.'

'What I can appreciate, Mr Mayor, is you going back to where you came from, unless you want that derby filled full of holes.'

Payne turned from Swearingen to Stuart. Then he looked at each man standing next to Stuart. He wondered why Curly Pike was here. Payne walked up to Stuart and spoke almost in a whisper.

'Zeke, don't let this escalate to violence.'

'I'm going to keep the peace. That's my job. That's the job you gave me last night.'

Payne looked at Ezra.

'Mr McPherson, please put a stop to this. If anyone can put a stop to this madness, you can. I know you can. Zeke will listen to you.'

'Zeke is going to keep the peace, just like he said. Sometimes it takes a little killing to keep the peace.'

'Well, damn, McPherson, I like your choice of words,' Rayburn said. 'That's pretty eloquent for a coward from Missouri.'

'Rayburn, you shouldn't talk to Mr McPherson like that,' Treutlin said. 'Mr McPherson, I consider it an honor to stand here in the street facing you. I mean, you're something of a legend. Any man who rode with Jesse James and lived to tell about it has to be considered a legend. Rayburn has told me all about your heroic exploits with the James gang. When I encountered you at night on Mr Swearingen's land, you took advantage of the darkness and held a gun on me. That was not kindly. Now you're not going to have such an advantage. Still, I consider it an honor to face you. I consider it an honor to kill you.'

McPherson, Swearingen thought. At night. On my land. I know what you're doing, McPherson. You may think I don't, but I do. And it ends now.

Payne stepped back and looked at both groups of men, at the revolvers clinging to their sides, at the shotgun in Marcus's hands. They won't listen, he thought. No matter what I say, they won't hear a word. He returned to his store and closed the door.

'I've come to get my son,' Swearingen said. 'You have no right to keep him.'

'He has turned himself in,' Stuart said. 'He says he had

a hand in the lynching of the Darton boy. He has confessed to a crime. It's up to Judge Henry and a jury to decide whether he goes free. The judge is out of town. I can't do anything till he gets back. That's the law, Mr Swearingen.'

'You young pup,' Swearingen said, 'don't quote the law to me. I know more law than you'll ever hope to know.'

'That may be true, Mr Swearingen, but Andrew stays put.'

'McPherson, talk some sense into him,' Swearingen said. 'For once, I agree with Payne. You can put a stop to this. Nobody has to die. You and I have seen our share of killing. We've seen too much of it. Neither one of us wants to see more, but it's about to come to that. So talk to him.'

'Zeke is the sheriff,' Ezra said. 'If he says Andrew is not going anywhere, then Andrew is not going anywhere. You and your men need to get back on your horses and ride out of here. Let the law handle this.'

'You're a fine one to talk about the law,' Rayburn said. 'A man who rode with Jesse James. How many trains have you robbed? How many banks have you held up? How many men have you killed? Of course, you did most of your killing before you turned coward and walked away from James.'

'That's enough, Rayburn,' Swearingen said. 'Look, Sheriff, consider who you've got standing beside you. Yeah, McPherson knows what he's doing. But what about that Pinkerton? He's just an old man.'

'This old man still knows how to fire a revolver,' Owen said.

'Maybe. And then there's a newspaper reporter. What does he know about gunfights? I don't think they have too many of them in Atlanta. Is he someone you want facing my men? And then there's Curly Pike. I don't know what the hell he's doing here. But if he has betrayed me, what makes you think he won't betray you? Once the shooting starts, he'll turn tail and run. I've seen men like him. I saw them at Gettysburg.'

Stuart's right hand trembled. He looked at each man facing him. Each man a gunfighter. Each man a killer.

'What you say may be true,' Stuart said. 'You may kill me, but I have to stand up for the law.'

'The town isn't paying you enough to stand here and get killed,' Swearingen said.

'It's not about money.'

The front door of the jail banged shut, but Ezra did not take his eyes off the men standing n front of him. Suddenly Andrew stood next to Curly. Luke was behind him.

'Son, are you all right?' Swearingen asked.

'Yes, Father, I'm fine.'

'Luke, why did you bring him out here?' Ezra asked.

'I need to talk to my father,' Andrew said. 'Please, Father, don't do this. I feel I have to pay. That Darton boy didn't do anything wrong. I should have stopped what happened. I've got to pay for it. Please understand.'

'No, son, I don't understand. You're a Swearingen. You have no business being in jail. You're just a little confused, that's all. Come on back to the ranch. Once you're back home for a few days, you'll be all right. You'll forget about all this.'

'No. For once I'm not confused. I know what I have to do.'

'Yeah, I know what he's going to do,' Curly said.

Ezra glanced quickly at Curly.

'Curly, keep your mouth shut. Let Zeke handle this.'

'I'm the only one who knows what Andrew's going to do,' Curly said.

'Curly, what are you talking about?' Andrew asked.

'Curly Pike, I've never thought you had an ounce of

sense,' Swearingen said. 'You're confirming all my suspicions.'

'Crazy, am I? You won't think I'm so crazy when Andrew stands in a courtroom and tells the whole world what he knows. Rayburn is the one who gunned down John Tisdale. Not only that, but—'

'Pike, you lyin' bastard!' Rayburn said, and he reached for his pistol.

'Rayburn, no!' Swearingen said.

Swearingen grabbed Rayburn's arm, but the foreman shook free and swung the pistol at Swearingen's head and knocked the big man to the ground.

CHAPTER SIXTEEN

Charlotte prepared supper in the kitchen. Fried chicken, her specialty. Jennifer set plates on the table. She kept looking at the front door, as if expecting Luke to walk in at any moment. Perhaps he would say that everything was all right. Everything had been worked out. No violence would occur, so she could rest easy. The clock on the mantel ticked, and the ticking had never seemed so loud.

'Charlotte, I'm scared.'

'Honey, it's going to be all right,' Charlotte said as she turned the chicken over in the skillet.

The chicken popped, and some of the grease landed on Charlotte's wrist.

'Ouch! I need to be more careful.'

The popping of the chicken was loud, but not as loud as the ticking of the clock. Jennifer almost dropped a plate. The ticking reverberated in her ears. She was thankful that Bobby was inside. He sat on the sofa and thumbed through another McGuffey Reader that Silas had brought home from the store. Silas turned the pages of the newspaper.

Pistol shots came quickly. Jennifer threw off her apron. She did not hear glass shattering, wood splintering, men moaning. All she heard were the shots.

'I have to go. Please look after Bobby.'

'Jennifer, please stay here—' Charlotte said.

'It's too dangerous!' Silas said, and he stood but did not attempt to block her. 'Don't go. Please! Don't go.'

'Ma, what's wrong?'

'I'll be back, Bobby. You do what your aunt and uncle say. Be a good boy.'

She ran into the late afternoon heat. Neighbors came onto their porches and looked up the street. Something bad was happening. They knew that, and they wondered what this woman from Charleston, this woman they hardly knew, this woman who had found shelter for her and her son in the home of her sister, was doing. They wanted to shout, to tell her to go back, but her feet moved too fast, and then she was gone.

The shots grew louder and she tried to run faster, to will her feet to move more quickly in the dust. She pulled her long cotton dress higher, yet she tripped on it. A horse thundered past. Ginevra Swearingen said nothing. She leaned forward in the saddle and went around the corner. And then the gunshots stopped.

Please, Lord, please let Luke be all right. Please, Lord, don't take him. I'm begging you, dear Lord. Please let him be all right.

She passed the red and white barber pole at the corner and stopped. One man she had never seen before ran past her. She would always remember the terror in his eyes. Close behind him was a man she would later learn was Curly Pike. He almost ran into her. He stumbled and fell. A bag of some sort fell onto the street, and he reached for it. He looked up at her, grabbed the bag, and ran.

Ginevra leaped from the saddle and ran to a man lying on the ground. Jennifer raised a hand to her eyes to shield the sun. Where was Luke? A man leaned against a hitching post. He held a pistol. A wounded animal, she thought.

That's what he looks like. Later she would be told the man's name was Treutlin, one of Swearingen's hired guns. She saw Marcus Stokesbury with a double-barrel shotgun. Treutlin lifted his pistol. Even as far away as she stood, she could see that his hand shook.

'Don't make me kill you,' Marcus said.

Jennifer saw Ezra. He was loading his pistol.

'Stokesbury, kill the son of a bitch!' Owen said.

Owen was on his knees, clutching his left shoulder. Treutlin raised the pistol higher.

'Please, drop the gun!' Marcus said. 'Don't make me kill you!'

Treutlin did not drop the pistol. Marcus squeezed one trigger. The force of the blast blew Treutlin away from the hitching post.

And then she saw Luke. He knelt beside Owen, and she ran to him.

Suddenly she felt someone's arm encircle her. The grip was tight, fierce.

'Not so fast, young lady. Where the hell you think you're going?'

'Jennifer!' Luke called.

She looked down at the arm and saw the blood. Ezra walked toward them. He came slowly. He held a pistol alongside his leg.

'Don't come any closer, McPherson,' the man said. 'I'll kill her.'

'Just like you killed John Tisdale.'

'I didn't kill him. Curly Pike was lying. I swear.'

'Just like you killed Harrison.'

'I didn't kill him. Why should I kill either one of them? But I'll kill her. You better believe me. You know I will. I'll kill her. I'm riding out of here.'

'Rayburn, you're not riding anywhere. Let the girl go.'

'Drop your pistol, McPherson. Drop it and I'll let her go.'

For what seemed like an eternity to Jennifer, no one spoke. Ezra and Rayburn seemed frozen. Then slowly Ezra, never taking his eyes off Rayburn, lay his Colt on the street. The grip around Jennifer's waist loosened, and she ran to Luke.

'You won't get far with that bullet hole in your side,' Ezra said.

'I'll get far enough.'

'You're wrong. You'll bleed to death.'

'If I'm going to die, I might as well take you with me.'

A gunshot dropped him to his knees. Surprise lit up his eyes. Blood dripped from the corner of his mouth. After the second gunshot, he collapsed and lay in the middle of the street. In the shadows of an overhang the girl stood, a Remington revolver in the firm grip of both hands. Meta Anderson stepped toward Rayburn.

'John, you can rest easy now. Rayburn won't kill nobody else. John, I've done what you wanted me to do.'

Ezra reached down and picked up his pistol and walked past Rayburn and took the Remington revolver from Meta. Her eyes, dazed and moist, still focused on the man at her feet.

'I had to do it,' she said. 'I had to. It's what John wanted.'

Suddenly a buggy thundered down the street and stopped. Doc Grierson, despite a sore, stiff back, walked quickly. In one hand he carried his black bag.

'Well, damnation. I'm gone for a couple of days to set a broken leg and treat the whooping cough and various and assorted other ailments, and while I'm gone, the town goes to hell. Luke, get this old man to my office before he bleeds to death.'

'Who you calling an old man, you old geezer?' Owen said.

'Sounds like he hasn't lost too much blood. I can't say that about these other men.'

Once on his feet Owen became faint and almost fell.

'I've got you,' Luke said. 'Just lean on me.'

Marcus went to the steps leading onto the sidewalk and sat, the shotgun in his lap. In the street lay gunmen, hired guns. He had heard stories about the great battles of the war – Shiloh, Antietam, Chickamauga, Gettysburg. He had heard stories about the awful killing. He had heard stories about the awful positions of dead bodies. He had heard stories not about the glory, but about the grotesque.

'Be thankful, boy, you didn't see it,' men told him, men who had been on the fields of death.

Now I've seen, he thought. Now I've been a part of it.

He stared at Treutlin.

'Why did you make me do it? Why?'

Ginevra was a statue in the middle of the street. She sat and cradled Andrew. Jennifer went to her and put her arm around her shoulder. The front of the mother's dress was red. She looked up at Ezra.

'They've killed my baby, Ezra. They've killed him.'

Doc Grierson lifted Andrew's wrist and checked for a pulse.

'Ma'am, he's not dead but he will be if we don't get to work.'

She held him tightly, as if she had not heard what he said.

'Gin, let me have him,' Ezra said.

She released her son and Ezra lifted him and carried him to Doc Grierson's office. The doctor and Jennifer followed. Swearingen was on his knees, blood on the side of his head.

'Richard, are you satisfied?' she asked.

When Ezra lifted Andrew, Swearingen stared at his son's blood-streaked face. He realized Andrew was just a boy.

One by one the few shopkeepers that had remained in town came onto the sidewalks. They examined the broken shards of glass and ran their fingers over the bullet-splintered wood in the side of buildings. They stared at the bodies. They stepped into the street to get a closer look and then returned to their shops. They would write about this day to their friends and families still living back East. We thought this kind of thing was behind us, they would write. It was like a war, a battle, and we wonder if the war is just beginning.

Slade hurried from the funeral parlor. He walked beside Owen and Luke.

'Don't look at me, you damn buzzard,' Owen said. 'I ain't dead.'

Stuart stood near the hitching post near Truetlin.

'I never thought I would kill a man,' Marcus said, and he wanted to fling the shotgun away. 'I begged him to put his gun down. Zeke, did you hear what I said to him? I begged him.'

'I heard. You did all you could do.'

'You didn't get hit, did you?'

'No. And I don't think I hit anyone. Ezra did most of the shooting before I even got my revolver out. Did you see how fast he was? He's as fast as I've heard, even faster. I never thought anyone could be that fast.'

Stuart noticed Meta. She still stood over Rayburn, and he left Marcus and approached her.

'You're Meta Anderson,' he said.

'Yes, Sheriff. Are you going to lock me up?'

'No. But I am going to take you home.'

'I know the way.'

'You shouldn't travel this late by yourself. I'm taking you. There ain't going to be any argument.'

They walked to the livery. Smitty waited.

'Sheriff, I sure am proud of you.'

'Thanks, Smitty. I wish I could say I'm proud of myself.'

Ezra, Andrew's bloody body in his arms, hurried past Eloise and Lawrence Byrd, who stood outside the newspaper office. He did not see them.

'Lawrence, take a good look at Ezra McPherson,' Eloise said. 'He's the last of a breed. I don't think we'll see his kind ever again.'

CHAPTER SEVENTEEN

Ginevra tucked the feather pillow behind Andrew's head. He smiled and looked at the passengers on the depot platform. They were ready to climb the metal steps of the Union Pacific passenger car bound for the East. Peter laid his hand on his brother's shoulder.

'You take care of yourself in New York,' Peter said.

'I don't think I'll be doing much of anything for a while. It's funny how things work out, isn't it?'

'How do you mean?'

'I'm the one who's returning to New York. You're the one who's staying here in Cheyenne.'

Andrew's face was pale. He coughed and closed his eyes.

'You just rest easy,' Peter said.

'I'm going to be on the platform for a few minutes,' Ginevra said. 'Do you need anything?'

'I'm fine.'

'I'll be right back. Don't leave without me.'

'Don't worry.'

Ginevra and Peter moved past passengers seeking seats and stepped onto the platform. She must be expecting

Father to come, Peter thought. I doubt there's much chance of that happening.

'Are you sure it's safe for him to travel?' he asked.

'Doc Grierson assured me it is. One thing is for certain – Judge Henry wants him to travel. Peter, I'm concerned about you and Anne on the ranch. Are you sure you want to stay?'

'We'll be fine. I'll find a good foreman.'

'I hope he's nothing like Rayburn. Peter, I don't know where your father is. I haven't seen him since the – since your brother was shot. I'm sure he's still in Wyoming. You see, his ranch is his kingdom. I don't think he's ready to abdicate his throne. One of these days you'll look out a window and see him coming. If he makes life difficult for you, come to New York.'

'Anne wants to stay here. She says Cheyenne is home.'

'Anne is a good girl. You're lucky.'

Ezra came around the corner and walked down the platform and removed his wide-brimmed black hat.

'Mrs Swearingen.'

'Mr McPherson.'

Ezra reached out and shook Peter's hand.

'I've heard you and your wife are staying here,' Ezra said.

'Yes, sir. I guess it sounds a bit crazy since I don't know anything about ranching.'

'You'll learn. A good foreman will help.'

'I was just telling Mother—'

The whistle blew and the locomotive hissed and steam rushed onto the far end of the platform. Ginevra kissed her son on the cheek.

'Goodbye, Mother. Take care.'

'You, too.'

Peter left the platform and disappeared around the corner of the depot.

149

'I was wondering if you would come to bid me a farewell.'

'I wish you would stay,' Ezra said.

'I can't. You heard what Judge Henry said.'

'Yes.'

Judge Henry was elderly. His appearance was that of a gentleman, from his neatly pressed dark blue suit to his thick white beard. Ezra sat next to Ginevra in the small courtroom. They were behind the table where Andrew and his attorney, Darrell Fitzsimmons, sat. To find an attorney, Ginevra had sought Ezra's help. A Virginian, Fitzsimmons had practised in Cheyenne many years.

'I knew John Tisdale,' Fitzsimmons told Ezra. 'I considered him a friend.'

The courtroom was hot. The Darton mother held young Jody Darton's hand and led him to the chair next to Judge Henry. Jody wore clean overalls that were thin in the knees. The dust had been cleaned off the shoes that were too big for him. The boy sat and glanced at the judge and then at the spectators, mostly homesteaders, who huddled at the back of the courtroom. Ezra could tell that Jody was scared.

'May I stand here with my son?' Mrs Darton asked.

'Yes, ma'am. Jody, there's nothing to be afraid of. This is not a formal trial. Nothing like that. Jody, this is what we call a hearing. The purpose is to see if we need to have a trial. I'm just going to ask you a question or two. Just pretend you and me are on a river bank fishing and talking. Do you like to fish, son?'

'Yes, sir. For catfish.'

'Well, me too. Nothing like fried catfish. So that's what we're pretending to do. We're fishing for catfish and I'm just asking a question or two. All right, let's get started. Do you see anyone at the table in front of you that you've seen before?'

'Yes, sir.'

'Will you point him out?'

Jody pointed at Andrew.

'When did you see him?'

'The day Cliff was hanged.'

'Was he in favor of hanging your brother?'

'No, sir.'

'How do you know?'

'He told the others my brother didn't look like a cattle rustler. And my brother wasn't a cattle rustler. He never rustled no cattle.'

'Yes, son, I understand.'

'He wanted my brother to have a chance to talk, but the others wouldn't listen. Then they hanged him.'

Jody bowed his head. He had promised himself that he would be a big boy and not cry. He had told his ma and pa that he would not cry. But suddenly he saw his brother swinging at the end of a rope, his feet kicking violently. And the tears came. Once they came, he could not stop them. His mother stood next to the chair and pulled him toward her.

'You've done real good, Jody,' the judge said. 'Mrs Darton, you may take him back to your chairs. Andrew Swearingen, please stand. I think your willingness to accept the blame for what happened to Cliff Darton is admirable. It's courageous. You did what you could to stop the lynching. You can't be held responsible. I don't see that it's going to do anybody any good to bind you over for trial. So I'm going to release you from jail. I want you to leave Cheyenne just as soon as Doc Grierson says it's all right for you to travel. I'm not going to say you can never return. But I will say you need to stay away for a good long while.'

'What kind of justice is this?' Jody's father asked, and he stepped toward the judge. 'Andrew Swearingen deserves what my son got!'

Ezra remembered the first time he saw the father. It was right after the lynching. He was thin and pale. He did not look at all healthy. In the courtroom his voice was surprisingly strong.

'Sir, that will be enough,' Judge Henry said, and the gavel came down hard on the oak table.

'This ain't no justice! How much money did Swearingen pay you?'

'If you don't shut your mouth, I'm going to hold you in contempt.'

'There's going to be war. The Swearingens will pay for what they did to my boy!'

Darton turned and he and his wife and Jody left the courtroom. The other homesteaders just stood and stared at the judge. Then they too filed through the door.

Again the locomotive hissed. Ginevra took Ezra's hand.

'I know you talked to the judge,' she said.

'What makes you think that?'

'I know.'

'I just asked him if he'd like a box of cigars at Christmas.'

She grinned and squeezed his hand.

'It's good to see you smile, Gin. It's something I haven't seen in a long time. When we were young, I always thought you had the most beautiful smile.'

'When we were young, we had so much to smile about. Ezra, you could come to New York.'

'Me in New York?'

'On second thought, you'd better stay.'

Again she smiled, but the smile quickly left.

'Before I go, I'll tell you what I told Peter. I feel certain Richard is still here in Wyoming. He has tried to build an empire, and he's not going to walk away from it. There's something I didn't tell Peter, though I suspect he knows. Richard is a violent, vindictive man. He will not take responsibility for anything that has happened. He will try to kill you, Ezra.'

The conductor approached and called, 'All aboard!'

'I've been told that Rayburn was going to kill Curly Pike,' she said. 'Andrew stepped in front of Curly to protect him.'

'He did.'

'That says something about my son.'

'Yes, it does.'

'When you think of me,' she said, 'will you remember love beneath a cottonwood tree, on a hilltop overlooking the Medicine Bow River, with dry-weather lightning off in the distant sky?'

'I will remember.'

He took her into his arms and felt the warmth of her body. He kissed her and in that moment he wanted to board the train with her and leave Cheyenne. Then his arms released her and she climbed the steps and went inside the car and sat at the window next to Andrew. The locomotive lurched forward. It moved away from the depot, into the burning sunlight, ready to cross the plains, ready to cross the heartland of America. He stood on the platform and watched the train grow smaller. The smokestack left a long trail of black smoke that hovered over the tracks and then vanished. He wondered if he would ever see her again. Probably not, he thought. He put his hat on and left the platform and walked down the street.

He came to the spot where the bodies had lain, where their blood had darkened the dust. For a moment he stopped. All about him shoppers walked the sidewalks. Men on horseback and men in buckboards rode up and down the street. They were going about their business as if the gunfight had never taken place.

Benjamin Payne stepped out of his store and raised his hand.

'Good morning, Deputy McPherson.'

Ezra nodded and headed toward the jail. Another man called to him. Lansing approached.

'What can I do for you?' Ezra asked.

'You've already done plenty. The name's Lansing. I own one of the cattle spreads. What you did here was quite an accomplishment.'

'It's over.'

'Do you actually think putting Andrew Swearingen on the eastbound will appease the homesteaders? They were looking for justice. Do you think they got what they were looking for?'

'The judge made his decision. Everybody has to abide by it, including the homesteaders. What's your point?'

'You said it's over. No, Deputy McPherson, it's not over. It's only beginning. I'm sure we'll meet again. Have a good day.'

Eloise walked along the sidewalk. Lansing went past her. Probably on his way to the gentlemen's club, she thought. A club for those who slither. In her hand she carried a pencil and small tablet.

'Good morning, Miss Endicott,' Ezra said.

'Beware of Lansing,' she said. 'He's the kind of man who likes nothing more than to stir up trouble.'

'I appreciate the advice. You know, the first time I saw you you carried a pencil and tablet.'

'I'm always on the lookout for news.'

'Do you expect to find any today?'

'I'm going to interview Mayor Payne. I want to know his plans for Cheyenne.'

'I'm sure he has them. You know, I detect a bit of coolness in the wind. It's coming out of the northwest.'

'I detect it too. Ezra, the deputy's star looks good on you. I believe you feel right at home here in Cheyenne.'

'At least for the time being.'

'I suppose you bade farewell to Mrs Swearingen.'

'I did.'

'That was thoughtful.'

'I'm a thoughtful person.'

'I'm sure you don't want to hear this – Ginevra Swearingen is no good for you, Ezra. You deserve better. Since you don't seem to know, I thought I would do my civic duty and make you aware.'

'I'm surprised a lady would say something like that.'

'The world is changing, Ezra McPherson. Haven't you noticed? These days ladies say all kinds of things, some of which you men may not want to hear.'

'I don't suppose you know of someone who is good enough for me.'

'Perhaps I do. And she has money. She doesn't have to marry to get it. Just remember what I've said.'

'I'll keep it in mind.'

Twilight fell slowly on the outskirts of Cheyenne, and Owen sat in the dark brown oak rocking chair on the Taylors' front porch. His left arm rested in a sling. He rocked back and forth and his shoulder ached, but he had been shot before. The pain would pass. Of course, it would let him know when rain was approaching. He looked at the red sky in the west. No chance of rain. But at least it was a bit cooler. The unmerciful heat was showing some pity.

'The wind definitely has a bit of chill,' Owen said. 'Before we know it, fall will be knocking on the door.'

Ezra sat on the top step and smoked a cigarette. Luke

and Jennifer were in the porch swing. Her small feet did not touch the floor. Silas and Charlotte sat in straight chairs.

'Charlotte, it was kind of you and Silas to take an old coot like me in to recuperate,' Owen said. 'I'm pretty much on the mend. I'll be out of your way in a day or two.'

'You're no bother at all,' Charlotte said.

'No need to rush things,' Silas said.

From the back of the house came Bobby's shouts. 'Bang! Bang! You're dead!'

'I wish he wouldn't do that,' Jennifer said.

'He's a boy,' Silas said. 'Boys like to shoot up the back yard. When they start shooting up the town, that's when we have to worry.'

'I know, but—'

'He'll be fine,' Luke said.

Marcus maintained an uncertain perch on the porch bannister. He had wired his editor in Atlanta that he was still pursuing the story. It was not time to leave Cheyenne. Wilcox had wired a response: 'I understand'. Wilcox probably wonders whether I will ever return, Marcus thought. He's a damn good editor. Maybe he's not Henry Grady. But he's damn close.

Marcus kept thinking about the newspaper in Kingston. He kept thinking about Eloise's encouragement. I just may buy it, he thought. I do love the *Constitution*, but I want to publish my own paper. That's probably something Wilcox won't understand. When I tell him my plans, I'm sure he'll be surprised, but he won't show it. In fact, I have a pretty good idea as to what he'll say.

'Just give me the McPherson story before you leave.'

Bobby circled the house, chasing desperadoes, firing his wooden rifle. He sought protection behind a bur oak. He fired his rifle again and again. And then he was gone.

'Where's our sheriff?' Owen asked.

'He's looking in on Meta Anderson,' Ezra said.

'Does she need looking in on?'

'Apparently Zeke thinks so.'

'Zeke's a fine fellow,' Silas said. 'I'm not sure if he's cut out to be a lawman, though.'

'He's sure not much of a shot,' Owen said. 'If he shot straighter, that gunslinger wouldn't have plugged me in the shoulder. That young lady he's looking in on is a far sight better shot than he is.'

'You're a good one to talk,' Ezra said.

'When I shoot, I need to concentrate. And it's hard to concentrate when I've got a bullet hole in me. This shoulder still hurts. I think Grierson did as much damage as the bullet did. Luke, did he seem to know what he was doing?'

'He's a skillful surgeon,' Luke said. 'You should have seen him. He operated quickly. He definitely knew what he was doing. Of course, he's probably had plenty of experience with that sort of thing.'

'I agree,' Silas said. 'I'm sure he's seen his share of bullet holes. Doctor Tisdale, I believe you deserve some congratulations.'

'Why is that?'

'From what Jennifer has told me, you did quite a job on Andrew Swearingen. Of course, a lot of homesteaders would probably say they wished he hadn't made it.'

'Let's not talk about . . . that,' Charlotte said.

'Well, it's true. And then there was the hearing. I've already heard plenty of grumbles in the store. The homesteaders aren't happy. They still talk about a war. Ezra, I'm sure you've heard the same thing.'

'Would anyone like some coffee?' Charlotte asked.

'I'll help,' Jennifer said.

'Marcus, what are your plans?' Luke asked.

'I'll be here for a few more days.'

'He's waiting to see if there's going to be a range war,' Owen said.

'After the gunfight, did you wire a story back to the paper in Atlanta?' Silas asked.

'Yes.'

'Did you include your role?' Ezra said.

'I didn't think it was important.'

'Not important?' Owen said. 'That man you killed was about to shoot Ezra. One thing I learned was that Ezra can't reload as fast as he once could. Anyway, whether you realize it or not, you saved Ezra's life.'

Marcus had not thought about it. A man on a bicycle rode down the street.

'When my shoulder heals, I'm going to get one of those things,' Owen said.

'When you're ready to buy, come see me,' Silas said. 'I can order you one.'

'Any word on Swearingen's whereabouts?' Luke asked.

'Not a word,' Ezra said. 'I thought he might have gotten on the train with Ginevra, but he didn't.'

'You should have gotten on that train,' Owen said. 'You let Ginevra get away not once, but twice. How many opportunities do you think you're going to have with that woman?'

'I don't need love advice from a Pinkerton detective.'

'Well, you need it from someone. Luke, talk some sense into this man's head.'

Marcus left the bannister and stared at the street. He smelled the coffee that was brewing, and the smell was good.

'I've been curious about something ever since it happened,' Marcus said, really to no one, for his eyes never left the street. 'Curly Pike – why do you think he ran? I thought he wanted to help. Somehow I never expected him to bolt and run the way he did.'

Ezra flipped the cigarette onto the ground, and Owen leaned back in the chair.

'I don't reckon he had much fight in him,' Owen said.

'Well, at least he identified John's killer,' Luke said. 'I came out here wanting to know what happened. For a while it looked like I wasn't going to find out anything. It looked like John's killer would go unpunished. I didn't expect to find out from Curly Pike, but I did. Now I know. Curly told us who did it.'

Ezra stood and turned toward Luke.

'Ezra, why do you have that strange look on your face?' Luke asked. 'You heard what Curly said. He told us who killed John. Ezra, what's the matter? We know.'

'Yes, you're right,' Ezra said. 'We know.'